COJ

ABER ✔ KT-233-563

Boggarts

Beta for Boggart

B
P ←— ripper

X ←— rank
Gregory ←— name

I – dangerous
X – hardly detectable

B Naturally bound boggart

B Artificially bound boggart

Ghosts/Ghasts

Y
X ←—

I – dangerous
X – hardly detectable

Gregory

Witches

O M ←—

M – malevolent
B – benign
U –

B000 000 006 4669

ABERDEEN LIBRARIES

Character profiles

Tom

Thomas Ward is the seventh son of a seventh son. This means he was born with certain gifts – gifts that make him perfect for the role of the Spook's apprentice. He can see and hear the dead and he is a natural enemy of the dark. But that doesn't stop Tom getting scared, and he is going to need all his courage if he is to succeed where twenty-nine others have failed.

The Spook

The Spook is an unmistakable figure. He's tall, and rather fierce looking. He wears a long black cloak and hood, and always carries a staff and a silver chain. Like his apprentice, Tom, he is left-handed, and is a seventh son of a seventh son.

For over sixty years he has protected the County from things that go bump in the night.

Alice

Tom can't decide if Alice is good or evil. She terrifies the local village lads, is related to two of the most evil witch clans (the Malkins and the Deanes) and has been known to use dark magic. But she was trained as a witch against her will and has helped Tom out of some tight spots. She seems to be a loyal friend, but can she be trusted?

Mam

Tom's mam always knew he would become the Spook's apprentice. She called him her 'gift to the County'. A loving mother and an expert on plants, medicine and childbirth, Mam was always a little different. Her origins in Greece were a mystery. In fact, there were quite a few mysterious things about Mam . . .

THE WARDSTONE CHRONICLES

THE SPOOK'S DESTINY

JOSEPH DELANEY

Interior illustrations by David Wyatt

RED FOX

THE SPOOK'S DESTINY
A RED FOX BOOK: 978 1 849 41106 6

First published in Great Britain by The Bodley Head,
an imprint of Random House Children's Books
A Random House Group Company

Bodley Head edition published 2011
Red Fox edition published 2012

1 3 5 7 9 10 8 6 4 2

Copyright © Joseph Delaney, 2011
Cover illustration © Talexi Taini, 2011
Interior illustrations copyright © David Wyatt, 2011

The right of Joseph Delaney to be identified as the author of this work has been
asserted in accordance with the Copyright, Designs and Patents Act 1988.

All rights reserved. No part of this publication may be reproduced, stored in a retrieval system,
or transmitted in any form or by any means, electronic, mechanical, photocopying,
recording or otherwise, without the prior permission of the publishers.

The Random House Group Limited supports the Forest Stewardship Council (FSC®),
the leading international forest certification organization. Our books carrying the FSC
label are printed on FSC®-certified paper. FSC is the only forest certification scheme
endorsed by the leading environmental organizations, including Greenpeace. Our paper
procurement policy can be found at www.**randomhouse**.co.uk/environment.

MIX
Paper from
responsible sources
FSC® C016897

Set in 10.5/16.5 Palatino by Falcon Oast Graphic Art Ltd

RANDOM HOUSE CHILDREN'S BOOKS
61–63 Uxbridge Road, London W5 5SA

www.**kidsatrandomhouse**.co.uk
www.**totallyrandombooks**.co.uk
www.**randomhouse**.co.uk

Addresses for companies within The Random House Group Limited can be found at:
www.randomhouse.co.uk/offices.htm
THE RANDOM HOUSE GROUP Limited Reg. No. 954009

A CIP catalogue record for this book is available from the British Library.

Printed and bound in Great Britain by CPI Group (UK) Ltd, Croydon, CR0 4YY

for Marie

THE HIGHEST POINT IN THE COUNTY
IS MARKED BY MYSTERY.
IT IS SAID THAT A MAN DIED THERE IN A
GREAT STORM, WHILE BINDING AN EVIL
THAT THREATENED THE WHOLE WORLD.
THEN THE ICE CAME AGAIN, AND WHEN IT
RETREATED, EVEN THE SHAPES OF THE
HILLS AND THE NAMES OF THE TOWNS
IN THE VALLEYS CHANGED.
NOW, AT THAT HIGHEST POINT ON
THE FELLS, NO TRACE REMAINS OF WHAT
WAS DONE SO LONG AGO,
BUT ITS NAME HAS ENDURED.
THEY CALL IT —

THE WARDSTONE.

CHAPTER 1
BEWARE THE JIBBER!

Driven by the gentlest of breezes, our small fishing boat was sailing slowly west, bobbing gently towards the distant shore. I was staring ahead towards the green hills of Ireland, trying to take in as much as I could before the light failed. In another twenty minutes it would be dark.

Suddenly there was a roaring, howling sound, and the fisherman looked up in alarm. From nowhere a great wind blew up. A black cloud raced towards us from the north, zigzag lightning flickering down into the sea, which was now boiling and surging so that the small boat rolled alarmingly. Our three dogs began to whimper. The usually fearless wolfhounds, Claw,

Blood and Bone, didn't like sea voyages at the best of times.

I was on my knees, clinging to the prow, cold pinching my ears, sea-spray stinging my eyes.

The Spook and my friend Alice were cowering down below the gunwales, doing their best to take shelter. The waves had suddenly become much bigger – unnaturally so, I thought. We seemed about to capsize. As we slid down into a trough, a gigantic wave, a sheer wall of water, came out of nowhere and loomed above us, threatening to smash our fragile craft to matchwood and drown us all.

But somehow we survived and rode up the wave to its crest. A torrent of hail came then – pebbles of ice, raining down onto the boat and us, beating at our heads and bodies with stinging force. Again lightning flashed almost directly overhead. I looked up at the mass of churning black cloud above us, and suddenly saw two orbs of light.

I stared up at them in astonishment. They were quite close together and made me think of two staring eyes.

Then, as I watched, they began to change. They *were* eyes – very distinctive eyes too, peering down from the black cloud. The left one was green, the right blue, and they seemed to glitter with malice.

Was I imagining it? I wondered. I rubbed my own eyes, thinking that I was seeing things. But no – they were still there. I was about to shout to get Alice's attention, but even as I watched, they faded away to nothing.

The wind dropped as suddenly as it had arisen, and within less than a minute the huge waves were no more. The sea was still livelier than it had been before the storm, though, and the wind was once more at our backs, driving us towards land at a much faster rate.

'Five minutes and I'll put you ashore!' cried the fisherman. 'There's a good side to everything, even a storm.'

I thought about the eyes in the cloud again. Maybe I'd only imagined them. It might be worth mentioning to the Spook later, but this wasn't the time.

'It was strange the way that storm came up so suddenly!' I shouted.

The fisherman shook his head. 'Not at all,' he said. 'You see strange things at sea, but that was just a squall. They often blow up out of nowhere. Mind you, that sea was something. Almost like a tidal wave. But this old tub is sturdier than she looks.' He looked quite pleased with himself. 'I need to be back well before dawn, and we've got a bit o' wind to fill our sails now.'

The Spook had paid him generously with almost the last of his money, but even so the fisherman had taken a big risk. We'd sailed away from the Isle of Mona about eight hours earlier, making the crossing west towards Ireland. We were refugees from the invasion of the County, and the Spook, Alice and I had spent many dangerous months on that island. Now the inhabitants of Mona were returning any refugees they found to the County – into the hands of the occupying forces. Intensive searches were being made. It had been time to get away.

'I hope we get a better welcome here,' said Alice despondently.

'Well, girl, it couldn't be much worse than last time,' said the Spook.

That was true enough. On Mona we'd been on the run almost immediately.

'You should have little trouble here!' shouted the fisherman, trying to make himself heard above the whine of the wind. 'Very few of your folk will have ventured this far, and it's a big island. A few more mouths to feed won't worry them much. You might find there's work for a spook too. Some call it the "Haunted Isle". It certainly possesses more than its fair share of ghosts.'

Spooks dealt with the dark. It was a dangerous trade, and I was in the third year of my apprenticeship to my master, John Gregory, learning how to deal with witches, boggarts and all manner of supernatural creatures. Ghosts usually posed little threat and were the least of our worries. Most didn't even know they were dead and, with the right words, could be persuaded to go into the light.

'Don't they have spooks of their own?' I asked.

'They're a dying breed,' said the fisherman. There was an awkward silence. 'I hear tell there are none working in Dublin, and a city like that is bound to be plagued by jibbers.'

'Jibbers?' I queried. 'What's a jibber?'

The fisherman laughed. 'You a spook's apprentice and don't know what a jibber is? You should be ashamed of yourself! You need to pay more attention to your lessons.'

I felt annoyed by his comments. My master was lost in thought and didn't seem to be listening to the fisherman. He had never mentioned a jibber, and I was sure there was no account of such things in his Bestiary, which was tucked safely away in his bag. He had written it himself; an illustrated record of all the creatures he'd encountered and heard of, with notes on how to deal with them. There was certainly no reference to a jibber in the 'Ghosts' section. I wondered if he even knew they existed.

'Aye,' continued the fisherman, 'I wouldn't like your

job. Despite its storms and moods, the sea is a far safer place to be than facing a jibber. Beware the jibber! Better to be drowned than driven mad!'

At that point the conversation came to an end: the fisherman brought us alongside a small wooden jetty that ran out into the sea from a bank of shingle. The three dogs wasted no time in leaping from the boat. We clambered out more slowly. We were stiff and cold after the voyage.

Moments later, the fisherman put out to sea again, and we made our way to the end of the jetty and up the shingle, our feet crunching on the stones. Anyone would be able to hear our approach from miles away, but at least they wouldn't be able to see us in the gloom. And in any case, if the fisherman was right, we should be in no danger from angry islanders.

There were dense clouds above and it was now very dark, but the shape of what we took to be a dwelling loomed up in front of us. It proved to be a dilapidated boathouse, where we sheltered for the night.

* * *

Dawn brought a better day. The sky had cleared and the wind had dropped. Although still chilly, the late February morning suggested the approach of spring.

The fisherman had called this the Haunted Isle, but its other name, the 'Emerald Isle', was hopefully more apt – though in truth the County was just as green. We were descending a grassy slope; below us lay the city of Dublin, its dwellings hugging both banks of a big river.

'What's a jibber?' I asked the Spook. As usual, I was carrying both our bags and my staff. He was striding along at a brisk pace, making it hard for Alice and me to keep up.

'I don't rightly know, lad,' he said, glancing back at me over his shoulder. 'It's probably the local name for something we're already familiar with – that's the most likely explanation. For example, what we call a boggart is known as a *bogle* or even a *bogeyman* in some parts of the world.'

There were many types of boggart, ranging from bloodthirsty rippers to relatively harmless hall-knockers that just thumped and banged and scared people. It was odd to think that some folk called them by different names.

I decided to tell my master what I'd seen in the storm the previous night. 'Remember when that squall hit us?' I said. 'I saw something strange in the dark cloud overhead – a pair of eyes watching us.'

The Spook came to a halt and stared at me intently. Most people would have been incredulous; others would have laughed openly. I knew that what I was saying sounded crazy, but my master was taking me seriously.

'Are you sure, lad?' he asked. 'We were in danger. Even the fisherman was scared – although he tried to play it down later. In situations like that the mind can play strange tricks on us. Our imaginations are always at work in that way. Stare at the clouds long enough, and you can see faces in them.'

'I'm sure it was more than just my imagination. There were two eyes, one green and one blue, and they looked far from friendly,' I told him.

The Spook nodded. 'We need to be alert. We're in a

land that's strange to us – there could be all sorts of unknown dangers lurking here.'

With that, he set off ahead again. I was surprised that Alice hadn't contributed anything to the conversation; she had a worried expression on her face.

Just over an hour later we smelled a whiff of fish on the air; soon we were threading our way through the narrow, congested streets of the city, heading towards the river. Despite the early hour, there was noisy hustle and bustle everywhere, people pushing their way through, street traders haranguing us from every corner. There were street musicians too – an old man fiddling and several young boys playing tin whistles. But despite the chaos, nobody challenged our right to be in the city. It was a far better start than we'd had in Mona.

There were plenty of inns, but most of them had notices in their windows saying that they were full. At last we found a couple with vacancies, but at the first the price proved too high. My master had scarcely any money left, and hoped to get us accommodation for three or four nights while we managed to earn some. At the second inn we were refused rooms without any real explanation. My master didn't argue. Some folks didn't like spooks; they were scared by the fact that they dealt with the dark and thought that evil things would never be far away.

Then, in a narrow back street about a hundred yards from the river, we found a third inn with vacancies. The Spook looked up at it doubtfully.

'No wonder they got empty rooms,' said Alice, a frown creasing her pretty face. 'Who'd want to stay here?'

I nodded in agreement. The front of the inn needed a good lick of paint, and two of the first-floor windows and one on the ground floor were boarded up. Even the sign needed attention; it was hanging from a single nail, and each gust of wind threatened to send it tumbling down onto the cobbles. The name of the inn was the Dead Fiddler, and the battered sign depicted a skeleton playing a violin.

'Well, we need a roof over our heads and we can't

afford to be too fussy,' said the Spook. 'Let's seek out the landlord.'

Inside, it was so dark and gloomy that it might have been midnight. This was partly caused by the boarded windows but also by the large building opposite, which leaned towards this one across the narrow street. There was a candle flickering on the counter opposite the door, and beside it a small bell. The Spook picked up the bell and rang it loudly. At first only silence answered his summons, but then footsteps could be heard descending the stairs, and the innkeeper opened one of the two inner doors and entered the room.

He was a thick-set, dour-looking man with lank greasy hair that fell over his frayed collar. He looked down in the mouth, defeated by the world, but when he saw my master, he took in the cloak, the hood and the staff, and instantly his whole demeanour changed.

'A spook!' he exclaimed eagerly, his face lighting up. 'To be sure, my prayers have been heard at last!'

'We came to enquire about rooms,' my master said.

'But am I to understand that you've a problem I could help you with?'

'You *are* a spook, aren't you?' The landlord suddenly glanced down at Alice's pointy shoes and looked a little doubtful.

Women and girls who wore pointy shoes were often suspected of being witches. That was certainly true of Alice; she'd received two years' training from her mother, Lizzie the bone-witch. She was my close friend, and we'd been through a lot together – Alice's magic had saved my life more than once – but my master was always concerned that one day she might again drift towards the dark. He frowned at her briefly, then turned back to the innkeeper.

'Aye, I'm a spook, and this is my apprentice, Tom Ward. The girl's called Alice – she works for me, copying books and doing other chores. Why don't you tell me why you need my services?'

'You sit yourselves down over there and leave your dogs in the yard,' said the landlord, pointing to a table in the corner. 'I'll get you some breakfast and then tell you what needs to be done.'

No sooner were we seated than he brought across another candle and set it down in the centre of the table. Then he disappeared into one of the back rooms, and it wasn't long before we heard the sizzle of a frying pan and a delicious aroma of cooking bacon wafted through the door.

Soon we were tucking into large steaming platefuls of bacon, eggs and sausages. The landlord waited patiently for us to finish before joining us at the table and beginning his tale.

'I haven't one paying customer staying here and it's been the same for nearly six months. They're too scared. Nobody will come near the place since it arrived – so I'm afraid I can't pay you in coin. But if you get rid of it, I'll let you have three rooms free of charge for a week. How does that sound?'

'Get rid of what?' demanded the Spook.

'Anyone who meets it goes stark staring mad within minutes,' the innkeeper told him. 'It's a jibber, and a very nasty one at that!'

CHAPTER 2
BLOOD EVERYWHERE

'What exactly is a jibber?' my master enquired.

'Don't you know?' asked the landlord, his face once more showing doubt.

'We don't have anything called a jibber back in the County, where I come from,' explained the Spook. 'So take your time and tell me all about it – then I'll know better what I'm dealing with.'

'A jibber often appears within a week of somebody killing themselves, and that's what's happened here,' the landlord told us. 'The chambermaid had been in my employment for over two years – a good hard-working girl, she was, and pretty as a picture. That was her downfall. She attracted someone above her station. I warned her, but she wouldn't listen.

'Well, to cut a long story short, he made her promises – ones that he had no intention of keeping. And even if he'd meant what he said, there's no way his family would have approved of their liaison. He was a young man with an inheritance to come and a good family name to uphold. I ask you – was he likely to marry a poor servant girl with not a penny to her name? He told her he loved her. She certainly loved him. But, predictably, it turned out badly. He married a titled lady – it seemed the marriage had been arranged for months. He'd been lying all the time, and when the girl found out her heart was broken. The silly creature cut her throat. Not an easy way to go. I heard her choking and coughing, and ran upstairs to see what the matter was. There was blood everywhere.'

'Poor thing,' murmured Alice, shuddering.

I nodded, trying to get the image of the chambermaid's terrible death out of my head. It was a big mistake to kill yourself, no matter how bad the situation seemed. But the poor girl would have been desperate, not really knowing what she was doing.

'There are still stains on the floorboards,' continued the landlord, 'and no amount of scrubbing will get 'em out. She took a long time to die. Got her a doctor, but he couldn't help. Doctors are useless, and that's a fact. I wouldn't give one the time of day. Anyway, she'd have gone to a pauper's grave, but she'd been a good worker, as I said, so I paid for her funeral myself. She'd been dead less than a week when the jibber arrived. The poor girl was hardly cold in her grave and—'

'What were the first signs of its arrival?' interrupted the Spook. 'Think carefully. It's important.'

'There were strange rappings on the floorboards – there was a rhythm to them: two quick knocks, then three slow ones, over and over again. After a few days, an icy chill could be felt at the spot where the poor girl had died – right above the bloodstains. A day later, one of my guests went mad. He jumped through the window and broke both his legs on the cobbles below. His legs will heal, but his mind is beyond repair.'

'Surely you weren't still using that room? No doubt

you warned him about the rappings and the cold spot?'

'He wasn't staying in the room where the girl died – that was a servant's room in the attic, right at the top of the building. A jibber haunts the very spot where a suicide occurs, and I assumed that it would stay there. Now they tell me that it can wander anywhere inside the building.'

'Why do they call the thing a *jibber*?' I asked.

'Because of the noise it makes, boy,' the landlord replied. 'It makes jibbering and jabbering noises. It natters and prattles away to itself – sounds that don't make any sense but are terrifying to hear.' He turned back to the Spook. 'So, can you sort it out? Priests can do nothing. This is a city full of priests, but they're no better than doctors.'

The Spook frowned. 'Now, as I said, I come from a different place – the County, which is a land across the sea to the east,' he explained. 'I have to admit that I've never heard of what you're describing. You'd have thought that news of something so odd would have reached us by now.'

'Well, you see,' said the landlord, 'jibbers are new to the city. They first started to appear about a year ago. They're like a plague. They were first sighted in the southwest, and have slowly spread east. The first cases reached the city just before Christmas. Some think they're the work of the goat mages of Kerry, who are always dabbling in dark magic. But who can say?'

We knew little about the Irish mages – only that they were in a state of constant war with some of the landowners. There was just a short reference to them in the Spook's Bestiary. They supposedly worshipped the Old God, Pan, in return for power. It was rumoured that human sacrifice was involved. It was a nasty business.

'Am I right in saying that this jibber of yours is only active after dark?' enquired the Spook.

The landlord nodded.

'Well, in that case we'll try to sort it out tonight. Would you mind if we took our rooms in advance of the job? We'd like to catch up on our sleep so that we're fit to face this jibber of yours.'

'By all means, but if you fail to sort it out, I'll expect to be paid for every day you stay here. I don't spend one minute in this place after dark – I sleep at my brother's. So, if it proves necessary, pay me in the morning.'

'That's fair enough,' said the Spook, shaking hands with the landlord to clinch the deal. Most folk didn't like to get too near to a spook, but this man was in serious financial trouble and grateful for my master's help.

We each chose a room, and spent the rest of the morning and early afternoon catching up on our sleep, having arranged to meet in the kitchen about an hour before dark. Mine was a troubled sleep: I had a terrifying dream.

I was in a forest. There was no moon, but the trees were glowing with an unearthly silver light. Alone and unarmed, I was crawling on all fours, searching for something that I needed very badly – my staff. Without it, I realized, I wouldn't survive.

It was just a few minutes to midnight, and I knew that something was coming after me then – something terrible. My mind was befuddled and I couldn't remember what this creature was, but I knew that it had been sent by a witch. She wanted revenge for something I'd done to her.

But what was wrong with me? Why couldn't I remember things properly? Was I already under some sort of spell? Somewhere in the distance, a church bell began to strike ominously. Petrified with fear, I counted each chime.

At the third one I leaped to my feet in panic and began to run. Branches whipped at my face, brambles snatched and scratched at my legs as I sprinted desperately through the trees towards the unseen church. There was something after me now, but it wasn't running through the undergrowth; it wasn't something on either two legs or four. I could hear the furious beating of gigantic wings.

I glanced back over my shoulder and my blood turned to water. I was being chased by an immense black crow, and the sight of it increased my terror. It was the Morrigan, the Old God of the Celtic witches, the bloodthirsty deity who pecked out the eyes of the dying. But I knew that if only I could reach the church, I'd be safe.

Why that should be I didn't know – churches weren't usually places of refuge from the dark. Spooks and their apprentices preferred to rely on the tools of their trade and a sound knowledge of the practical defensive steps that could be taken. Nevertheless, I knew that I had to reach the church – or die and lose my soul to the dark.

I tripped over a root and sprawled headlong. I struggled to my knees and looked up at the black crow, which had alighted on a branch, making it creak and bend under its weight. The air shimmered in front of me, and I blinked furiously to clear my vision. When I could finally see, I was confronted by a terrible sight.

In front of me stood a tall figure wearing a black dress that came down almost to the ground. It was splattered with blood. The figure was female from the neck downwards, but she had the huge head of a crow, with cruel beady eyes and an immense beak. Even as I watched, the crow's head began to change. The beak shrank, the beady eyes softened and widened until the head was fully human. I suddenly realized that I knew that face! It was that of a witch who was now dead – the Celtic witch that the spook Bill Arkwright had once killed in the County. I'd been training with Arkwright, and had seen him throw a dagger into this witch's back; then he'd fed her heart to his dogs to make sure she couldn't come back from the dead. Bill had been ruthless in his treatment of witches – much harder than my master, John Gregory.

Or was it her? I had seen that witch close to and I was sure that both her eyes had been the same colour. And in that moment I knew that none of this was real. I was having a bad dream – and it was one of the very worst kind: a lucid nightmare where you're trapped and cannot escape, cannot wake up. It was also the same one that I'd been having for months – and each time it happened it was more terrifying.

The witch was walking towards me now, her hands outstretched, talons ready to rend the flesh from my bones.

I fought to wake myself up. It was a real struggle to break free. I opened my eyes and felt my fear gradually fall away. But it was a long time before I calmed down. I was wide-awake now and couldn't get to sleep again. It didn't leave me in the best state of mind to face a jibber – whatever that might be.

We met down in the kitchen, but we weren't planning to eat anything substantial. We were about to face the dark, so the Spook insisted that we fast, managing with just a little cheese to sustain us. My master missed his favourite crumbly County cheese, and wherever we happened to be, he was always complaining that the local fare wasn't a patch on it. But on this occasion he nibbled in silence before turning to me with a question.

'Well, lad, what are your thoughts on all this?'

I gazed into his face. It looked as if it had been chiselled from granite, but there were new deeper lines on his brow, and his eyes were tired. His beard had been grey from the moment I first saw him, almost three years ago, when he visited my dad's farm to talk about my apprenticeship. However, there had been a mixture of other colours in there too – mostly reds, browns and blacks; now it was entirely grey. He was looking older – the events of the past three years had taken their toll.

'It worries me,' I said. 'It's something we've never dealt with before, and that's always dangerous.'

'Aye, it is that, lad. There are too many unknowns. What exactly is a jibber, and will it be vulnerable to salt and iron?'

'There may be no such thing as a jibber,' said Alice.

'And what do you mean by that, girl?' demanded my master, looking annoyed. He no doubt thought that she was putting her nose where it didn't belong; meddling in spook's business.

'What if it's the spirit of each dead person that's somehow trapped and causing the problem?' she said. 'Dark magic could do that.'

The frown left the Spook's face and he nodded thoughtfully. 'Do the Pendle witches have such a spell?' he asked.

'Bone-witches have a spell that can bind a spirit to its own graveside.'

'Some spirits are bound like that anyway, girl. We call them *graveside-lingerers*.'

'But these don't just linger, they scare people,' Alice pointed out. 'The spell is often used to keep people away from a section of a churchyard so that witches are able to rob the graves and harvest the bones undisturbed.'

Bone-witches collected human bones to use in their type of magic. Thumb-bones were particularly prized. They boiled them up in a cauldron to obtain magical power.

'So, taken a step further, if these are trapped spirits, they're somehow being forced to drive people to the edge of madness. That all makes sense, but how and why is it spreading?' my master asked.

'If it is a spell,' Alice said, 'then it's out of control –

almost as if it's developed an energy of its own, spreading its evil, working its way east. Bony Lizzie once cast a powerful spell that got out of control. It was the first time I'd ever seen her scared.'

The Spook scratched at his beard as if something wick were crawling there. 'Aye, that makes sense,' he agreed. 'Well, I reckon we should visit the place where the poor girl killed herself first. I'll need the lad with me, so no doubt you'll be joining us too, girl.'

That last sentence was spoken with an edge of sarcasm. Alice and I were in a very bad predicament and he could do nothing about it. The previous year, in order to save the lives of many people, including the Spook and Alice, I'd sold my soul to the Fiend – the Devil himself, the dark made flesh. He had been summoned to earth by a gathering of the Pendle witch clans, and was now growing ever more powerful: a new age of darkness had come to our world.

Only Alice's dark magic now prevented the Devil from coming to collect my soul. She'd put three drops of her blood and three drops of mine together in what was called a 'blood jar'. I carried it in my pocket, and now the Fiend couldn't come near me – but Alice had to stay close by in order to share its protection.

There was always a risk that somehow I might get separated from the jar and be beyond its protective spell. Not only that: when I died – whether that was six or sixty years hence – the Fiend would be waiting to claim what belonged to him and would subject me to an eternity of torment. The only way out was to somehow destroy or bind him first. The prospect of the task weighed heavy on my shoulders.

Grimalkin, the witch assassin of the Malkin clan, was an enemy of the Fiend; she believed that he could be bound in a pit if he was pierced with silver-alloy spikes. Alice had made contact, and she had agreed to join us in order to attempt this. But long weeks had passed, and there had been no further communication from Grimalkin: Alice feared that, invincible though she was, something had happened to her. The County was occupied by foreign troops – maybe they had moved against the Pendle witches, slaying or imprisoning them. Whatever the truth, that blood jar was as important as ever.

Soon after dark, carrying a candle, the Spook led us up to the attic – the small cramped room right at the top of the inn where the poor servant girl had lived and died.

The bed had been stripped of its mattress, sheets and pillows. At the side of the bed nearest the window, I saw dark bloodstains on the floorboards. The Spook set his candle down on the little bedside table, and the three of us made ourselves as comfortable as possible on the floor just in front of the closed door. Then we waited. It was reasonable to expect that if the jibber was in need of victims tonight, it would come for us. After all, there was nobody else staying at the inn.

I'd filled my pockets with salt and iron – substances that usually worked against boggarts and, to a lesser extent, witches. But if Alice's theory was correct and we were dealing with a trapped, dangerous spirit, salt and iron would be ineffective.

We didn't have long to wait before the jibber arrived.

Something invisible began to rap on the floorboards. There were two quick knocks, then three slow ones. It happened over and over again, and my nerves were on edge. Next the candle flickered and there was a sudden chill in the air; I had an even colder feeling inside – the warning that a seventh son of a seventh son often receives when something from the dark approaches.

Directly above the bloodstains a column of purple light appeared; the sound that emanated from it confirmed that the jibber had been well named. The voice was high and girlish and sibilant. It jabbered nonsense, jarring my ears, making me feel uncomfortable and slightly dizzy. It was as if the world had tilted and I was unable to keep my balance.

I sensed the malevolence of the jibber: it wanted to hurt me very badly. It wanted my death. No doubt the Spook and Alice could hear the same disturbing sounds, but I glanced right and left, and neither was moving; they were just staring, wide-eyed, at the column of light as if transfixed.

But despite my dizziness I *could* move, and I decided

to act before the jabbering got right inside my head and made me do exactly what it wanted. I rose to my feet and strode forward, plunging my hands into my breeches pockets: my right hand seized salt, my left iron filings. I flung both handfuls at the column of light.

The substances came together perfectly, right on target. It was a good shot. The bad news was that nothing happened. The column continued to shimmer, and particles of salt and iron fell harmlessly and ended up scattered across the floorboards beside the bed.

Now the jibbering started to hurt. It felt as if sharp pins were being driven into my eyes and a band of steel was tightening across my forehead, slowly crushing my skull. I felt panic rising within me. At some point I would no longer be able to tolerate the pain. Would I be driven to madness? I wondered. Pushed to do something suicidal to end my torment?

With a shock, I realized something else then. The jabbering wasn't just meaningless prattling. The speed and sibilance had fooled me at first. This was the Old Tongue; a pattern of words. It was a spell!

The candle suddenly guttered out, plunging us in darkness – though the purple light was still visible. All at once I found that I was unable to move. I wanted to leave this claustrophobic attic where that poor girl had killed herself, but I couldn't – I was rooted to the spot. I felt dizzy too, and lost my balance. I tottered and fell hard onto my left side. I was aware of a sharp pain, as if I'd fallen on a stone.

As I struggled to rise, I heard another voice – a female voice, also chanting in the Old Tongue. This second voice grew louder while the first quickly died down until it had faded away altogether. To my relief, the jibbering had stopped.

Then I heard a sudden anguished cry. I realized that the second voice was Alice's – she'd used a spell of her own to end the jibber. The spirit of the girl was now free, but in torment. It knew that it was dead and trapped in Limbo.

Now there was a third voice, deeper, male – one that I knew well. It was the Spook.

'Listen, girl,' he said. 'You don't have to stay here . . .'

Befuddled as I was, for a moment I thought he was talking to Alice; then I understood that he was addressing the spirit of the dead girl.

'Go to the light,' he commanded. 'Go to the light now!'

There was a wail of anguish. *'I can't!'* cried the spirit. *'I'm lost in the mist. I can't find my way.'*

'The way is in front of you. Look carefully and you'll see the path to the light.'

'I chose to end my life. That was wrong, and now I'm being punished!'

It was always much harder for suicides and those who had died sudden violent deaths to find their way to the light. They sometimes wandered within the mists of Limbo for years. But it *could* be done. A spook could help.

'You are punishing yourself unnecessarily,' my master told the girl's spirit. 'There's no need. You were unhappy. You didn't know what you were doing. I want you to think very carefully now. Have you a happy memory of your earlier life?'

'Yes. Yes. I have lots of happy memories . . .'

'Then what's the happiest one – the happiest one of all?' he demanded.

'I was very young, no more than five or six years old. I was walking across a meadow, picking daisies with my mother on a warm sunny morning, listening to the droning of the bees and the singing of the birds. Everything was fresh and bright and filled with hope. She made a chain out of the daisies and put it on my head. She said I was a princess and would one day meet a prince. But that's just foolishness. Real life is very different. It can be cruel beyond measure. I met a man who I thought was like a prince, but he betrayed me.'

'Go back to that moment. Go back to the time when the future still lay ahead, full of warm promise and hope. *Concentrate,*' the Spook instructed. 'You are there again now. Can you see it? Can you hear the birds? Your mother is beside you, holding your hand. Can you feel her hand?'

'Yes! Yes!' cried the spirit. *'She's squeezing my hand. She's taking me somewhere . . .'*

'She's taking you towards the light!' exclaimed the Spook. 'Can't you see its brightness ahead?'

'I can see it! I can see the light! The mist has gone!'

'Then go! Enter the light. You're going home!'

The spirit gave a sigh full of longing, then suddenly laughed. It was a joyful laugh, followed by utter silence. My master had done it. He had sent her to the light.

'Well,' he said ominously, 'we need to talk about what's happened here.'

Despite our success, he wasn't happy. Alice had used dark magic to free the girl's spirit from the spell.

CHAPTER 3
THE VISITOR

Down in the kitchen, we ate a light supper of soda bread and gammon. When we'd finished, the Spook pushed his plate aside and cleared his throat.

'Well, girl, tell me what you did.'

'The maid's spirit was bound by a dark spell of compulsion,' said Alice. 'It was trapped within the inn and forced to utter a Befuddle spell that drives anyone who hears it to the edge of madness. Scares them so much, it does, they'll do anything to get away.'

'So what *exactly* did you do?' demanded the Spook impatiently. 'Leave nothing out!'

'I used what Bony Lizzie once taught me,' Alice replied. 'She was good at controlling the dead. Once she'd got what she wanted from them – so long as they hadn't tried too hard to resist, she let them go. She needed another spell to release them. It's called *avaunt* – an old word for "be gone".

'So, despite all my warnings against it, you used dark magic again!'

'What else was I supposed to do?' Alice said, raising her voice in anger. 'Salt and iron ain't going to work! How could it when you were dealing with a young girl's tortured spirit rather than something from the dark? And soon we'd have all been in real trouble. So I did what I had to do.'

'Good came out of it too,' I said in support of Alice. 'The girl's spirit has gone to the light and the inn is once again safe.'

The Spook was clearly deeply worried but had little more to say. After all, he had already compromised his principles by allowing us to keep the blood jar. Sensing that his silence was mostly directed at her, Alice got to her feet and stamped off up the stairs to her room.

I looked at my master; I felt sad when I saw the hurt

and dismay in his eyes. Over the past two years a rift had gradually come between the three of us because of this use of dark magic. I had to try and make amends, but it was hard to know what to say.

'At least we dealt with the jibber,' I said. 'I think I'll write it up in my notebook.'

'Good idea, lad,' the Spook said, his face brightening a little. 'I'll make a fresh entry in my Bestiary too. Whatever happens, we need to record the past and learn from it.'

So while I jotted a brief account of what had happened in my own notebook, the Spook pulled the Bestiary – the only book that had survived the burning of his house and library in Chipenden – from his bag. For a while we both wrote in silence, and by coincidence finished our records at almost the same moment.

'I'll be glad when the war's over and it's safe to return to Chipenden,' I said. 'Wouldn't it be nice to get back to our normal routine . . .'

'Aye, lad, it would. I certainly miss the County, and I'm looking forward to rebuilding that house of mine.'

'It won't be the same without the boggart, will it?' I commented.

The boggart had been a mostly invisible resident, occasionally appearing as a large ginger tom cat. It had served the Spook well in many ways, and had guarded the house and garden. When the house was burned down and the roof collapsed, the pact between my master and the boggart had ended. It had been free to leave.

'It certainly won't. We'll have to do our own cooking and cleaning, and you'll be making the breakfasts. My poor old stomach will find that hard to cope with,' said the Spook with the faintest of smiles. He always used to joke about my poor cooking, and it was good to see him attempting it again.

He looked a little more cheerful, and soon after that we went to bed. I felt nostalgic for our old life, and wondered whether it had now gone for ever.

However, the night's terrors weren't over yet. Back in my room I made a horrific discovery.

I put my left hand into the pocket of my breeches and

immediately realized what had caused the pain when I'd fallen on my side. *It had been the blood jar.*

Was it damaged? My heart sank into my boots. With a trembling hand I carefully withdrew the small jar from my pocket, carried it over to the candle and examined it. I shuddered with fear. There was a crack running along almost half its length. Was the jar now in danger of breaking? I wondered.

Close to panic, I went next door to Alice's room and knocked softly. When she opened it, I showed her the jar. At first she looked as alarmed as I was, but after examining it thoroughly she smiled reassuringly.

'It seems all right, Tom. Just a fine crack, it is. Our blood's still inside, which means we're safe from the Fiend. They're tough jars, those, and don't break easily. We're still all right, so don't you worry.'

I went back to my room, relieved to find that we'd had such a lucky escape.

The word soon spread around the city that there was a spook who could deal with a jibber.

So while we enjoyed the payment for our success – a week's stay at the inn – we were visited by others seeking our help.

The Spook refused to work with Alice again, but grudgingly allowed me to do so. So the night after our first visitation, Alice and I set out to deal with another jibber, this one plaguing the back workroom of a watchmaker's premises. The man had fallen into debt and had killed himself late one night after drinking too much wine. His relatives needed to sell the shop, but couldn't do so with a jibber in residence.

The encounter mirrored the first one at the inn almost exactly. After the rhythmic raps, a column of light appeared, and the spirit began its deadly work. However, it had hardly begun to jibber and jabber at us before Alice countered it with a spell. She did better than me, shutting it up quickly; for my part, I needed three attempts afterwards to send the spirit of the watchmaker to the light. It was no easy task: he'd had a difficult life, always counting his money and worrying about losing it. He didn't have many happy memories that I could draw upon. But at last I managed it, and his spirit was free.

But then something happened that filled me with dismay. Beside the workbench I saw a shimmer, and a column of grey light appeared. It seemed that another spirit had joined us. And there, close to the top of the column, was a pair of eyes glaring at me with extreme malice. One was green and the other blue; they looked very like the ones that I had seen in the storm cloud, and I stepped back in alarm.

Then the column of light shimmered and a woman stood before us. She wasn't present in the flesh – she was translucent, the candle on the workbench behind visible through her dark gown; it was her image projected from somewhere else. Suddenly I recognized her face. It was the witch that Bill Arkwright had killed.

I looked again, and with a stab of fright realized that this was the witch from my recurring dream.

'I hope you enjoyed my storm!' she cried, a gloating expression in her strange eyes. 'I could have drowned you then, but I'm saving you for later. I have something else in mind! I've been waiting for you, boy! With jibbers to be dealt with, I knew you'd show up. How do you like them? It's the best spell I've cast for many a long year.'

I didn't reply, and the witch's eyes swivelled towards Alice. 'And this is Alice. I've been watching the pair of you. I've seen what good friends you are. Soon you'll *both* be in my clutches.'

Angrily I stepped forward, placing myself between the witch and Alice.

She gave an ugly leer. 'Ah! I see that you care for her. Thank you for that, boy. You've confirmed what I suspected. Now I know another way to hurt you. And hurt you I will. I'll certainly pay you back many times over for what you've done!'

The image rapidly faded, and Alice came to my side. 'Who was that, Tom?' she asked. 'She seemed to know you.'

'Remember those eyes I saw in the cloud during the storm? It was her. Her face was that of the Celtic witch slain by Bill Arkwright.'

43

'I think we're both in danger. She has powerful magic – I can sense it,' Alice said, her eyes wide. 'Responsible for the jibbers, she is. She must be really powerful to do that.'

Back at the inn, we told the Spook of our encounter with the image of the witch.

'It's dangerous, being a spook,' he said. 'You could stop dealing with jibbers, but that would mean that many people would be harmed – innocent people who could be saved if you did your job bravely. It's up to you. The witch is an unknown quantity – someone to be treated with great caution. I wouldn't blame you for walking away. So what will you do?'

'We'll carry on – both of us,' I said, nodding towards Alice.

'Good lad – I thought that would be your answer . . . It still saddens me to think that the only way we can get rid of jibbers is by using dark magic,' my master added. 'Maybe things are changing, though. Maybe in the future that will be a new way for a spook to fight the dark, using the dark against itself. I don't hold with it myself, but I'm from a different generation. I belong to the past, but you're the future, lad. You'll face new and different threats, and deal with them in a different way.'

So Alice and I continued with our work, and in the space of six days, together we freed two inns, another shop and five private houses from jibbers. Each time, Alice countered the spell, and I then talked the freed spirit out of Limbo and into the light. Each time we felt apprehensive, but the witch didn't appear again. Was she bluffing and just trying to scare me away? But I had my job to do.

In contrast to the County, it seemed that the custom in Ireland was to pay someone immediately a job was completed, so we had plenty of money in our pockets. Then we had a visitor – someone who arrived on the seventh day, sending us off on a different course.

We were sitting at our usual table having breakfast. The inn still had no other customers, but the landlord was confident that the situation would soon change and had hinted that our departure would hasten the arrival of his first paying guest. Our presence here was now widely known, and although the inn was no longer haunted, few people would really wish to take a room in a place where a spook was staying. My master understood that, and we'd already decided to move our quarters later that day, probably heading south of the river Liffey, which divided the city.

I was just swallowing my last piece of bacon and mopping up my egg yolk with a wedge of buttered bread when a stranger entered the room from the street. He was a tall, upright man with white hair and a contrasting black beard and moustache. That alone was enough to earn him a second glance on any of the teeming Dublin thoroughfares; but add to that his clothes – a formal knee-length coat, neatly pressed black trousers and expensive boots, which marked him out as a gentleman of the first rank – and all eyes would have marked his passing. He also carried an ivory walking stick with a white handle in the shape of an eagle's head.

The landlord rushed across to greet him, bowing low before welcoming him into the inn and offering him the best room. But the stranger was barely listening to his host; he was staring across at our table. Wasting no time, he came across and addressed the Spook.

'Have I the pleasure of speaking to John Gregory?' he asked. 'And you must be Tom Ward,' he added, looking at me. He gave just a curt nod in Alice's direction.

The Spook nodded and got to his feet. 'Aye, that's me,' he said. 'And that's my apprentice. Are you here to ask for our help?'

The man shook his head. 'On the contrary, I am here to offer *you* assistance. Your success in ridding the city of many of its troublesome apparitions have brought you to the attention of a powerful and dangerous group. I speak of the goat mages of Staigue. We have our own spies, and they tell me that the mages have already dispatched assassins to this city. Being servants of the dark, they cannot tolerate your presence in our land. That is why the few remaining Irish spooks avoid the main towns and never settle in one place for more than a couple of days.'

The Spook nodded thoughtfully. 'We'd heard that they were a dying breed. What you say makes sense, but why should you wish to help us? By doing so, won't you be putting yourself at risk?'

'My life is permanently at risk,' said the man. 'Allow me to introduce myself. I am Farrell Shey, the leader of the Land Alliance, a league of landowners who have been at war with the mages for many years.'

In addition to what I'd read in the Spook's Bestiary, while working with Bill Arkwright I'd met a landowner who'd fled Ireland to escape the mages. It had done him no good. They'd sent one of the Celtic witches to slay him in his County refuge, and she had been successful, despite our best efforts to save him.

'Well, in that case, we would certainly welcome your assistance,' said the Spook.

'And in return,' Shey said, 'you may be able to use your expertise to help us. A dangerous few months lie ahead – ones which some of us will be hard-pressed to survive: the goat mages are preparing for their next ritual in Killorglin – so we must delay no further. Gather your things together and I'll get you out of the city immediately.'

We did as he instructed, and within a few minutes we'd taken our leave of the grateful landlord and were following Shey through a number of narrow alleyways, emerging onto a side street where a large carriage was waiting. Drawn by a team of six horses, it seemed to be made for speed, and its appearance was not deceptive. The coach driver was smartly dressed in green livery, and in attendance was a large black-bearded man with a sword at his belt, who bowed to Shey and opened the carriage doors for us before taking his place beside the driver.

Seated in comfort and hidden from the gaze of the curious by lace curtains, we had soon crossed the river and were heading west out of the city; the *clip-clop* now became a rhythmical thunder of pounding horses' hooves.

Alice turned towards me, and as our eyes met, I guessed that she was thinking the same thing as me:

this had all happened too fast. This Farrell Shey was used to being in command, and it had taken little persuasion to make us follow him. Just what were we getting ourselves into?

'Where are we bound?' asked the Spook.

'We're making for Kerry in the southwest,' Shey replied.

'But isn't that where the goat mages are based?' I said, starting to feel more than a little uneasy.

'It is indeed,' he answered. 'But we live there too. It is a beautiful but dangerous part of this fair island. And sometimes, in order to counter a threat, you have to go out boldly and face it. Would you rather have died in the city, waiting for the assassins to come for you? Or would you come and place your strength alongside ours in an attempt to end the power of the mages for ever?'

'We will add our strength to yours,' answered the Spook. 'Don't doubt that.'

Alice and I exchanged another look. The Spook had clearly made his decision.

'I've fought the dark all my life,' he told Shey, 'and I will do so until my dying day.'

All that day the carriage took us west, stopping only twice to change horses. The dogs travelled with us, occasionally running alongside to stretch their legs. Then the roads became narrower and the pace slowed considerably. By now, we could just make out snow-capped mountains in the far distance.

'Those are the mountains of Kerry; my home lies on the peninsula of Uibh Rathach,' said Shey. 'But we won't be able to reach it tonight. There's an inn ahead that we can make secure.'

'So we are in danger already?' asked the Spook.

'There is always danger. We'll have been followed from the city, and our enemies will be lying both ahead and behind us. But don't worry – we are well prepared.'

The place where we were to stay was situated on the edge of a wood and reached by a single narrow track. In fact it had no sign hanging outside, and although

Shey had called it an 'inn', it looked more like a private house commandeered to provide a refuge in a dangerous location.

That night, after walking the dogs, we dined well on generous portions of a potato and onion stew, rich with pieces of succulent mutton. As we ate, my master started to question Shey about the goat mages. He already knew the general answers to some of his questions, but that was the Spook's way: what Shey told him could also contain important new information that might make the difference between victory and defeat. Our survival could depend on what we were able to learn here.

'You mentioned that the goat mages are preparing for their ritual in Killorglin . . . ?' he asked.

'That's correct,' Shey replied, stroking his black moustache. 'That always brings a crisis.'

'But it's still winter, and I'd heard that the ceremony took place in August . . .'

'They now assemble twice a year,' Shey answered. 'It was once an annual late-summer event, held at what is known as the Puck Fair. They tether a mountain goat upon a high platform and leave it there; their dark rituals end in human sacrifices. The object is to persuade the god Pan to enter the body of the living goat. If he does so, their magic is made more powerful and they can hunt down and kill their enemies; but if the magic fails, it is our turn to pursue them.

'In their efforts to defeat us, they now try to invoke the god twice a year – in both March and August. Last year they failed on both occasions, but in all their long history of dealing with the dark they have never done so three times in a row.

'Additionally, they have a new leader – a dangerous fanatic called Magister Doolan who'll stop at nothing to achieve his aims. He's a bloodthirsty wretch who delights in the name of the "Bantry Butcher". He was born on the shores of Bantry Bay to the south, and was actually an apprentice butcher before he discovered his talent for the dark arts. But he hasn't lost his skill with knives. He kills people for the love of it, cutting off their fingers and toes one by one; killing

53

them with a hundred cuts to prolong their deaths, before finally chopping off their heads.

'So this is a time of great danger for us. We must assume that next month, unless we can stop them, they will summon Pan and acquire even more deadly power.'

'I've pledged my help – but how would you normally try and stop them?' asked the Spook.

'We've waged this war against the mages for centuries: our usual method is to use force of arms – though we've had limited success. They have an invulnerable refuge in the ring fort at Staigue, but the majority must venture out for the ceremony in Killorglin. So we often harry them on the way or attack them in the town itself. In the past, such attempts have only delayed the mages, but when their magic fails, we've then managed to kill a good many of them before they can return to the fort.'

'Do you know *why* they go to Killorglin?' my master wondered. 'Why there? Why don't they just perform the ceremony in the safety of their fort?'

Shey shrugged. 'We think that the site of the market in Killorglin is important: it's a place where natural dark power emerges from the earth. As far as we know they have never attempted the ritual elsewhere . . .'

That made sense. There were indeed special places on earth where the practice of dark magic was made easier: the whole County was a haven for boggarts. Within its boundaries there were sites of great potency, especially around Pendle Hill. Despite the flowing streams, which they could not easily cross, Pendle had attracted several large clans of witches.

'Can't the mages be driven from their refuge once and for all?' asked my master.

'That's impossible,' Shey replied. 'The Staigue fort is a formidable place, built by an ancient people who inhabited this island over two thousand years ago or more. To attempt to storm it would cost us too dearly. In practical terms it's invulnerable.'

'What about the Celtic witches?' I asked. 'Do you have any problems with them, Mr Shey?'

I was thinking of the eyes in the cloud and the witch

who had threatened us after we'd dealt with the jibber. Celtic witches were supposed to be allies of the mages.

'They sometimes act as spies for the mages but do not form clans. We're dealing only with the odd isolated witch – they're an occasional nuisance rather than the serious threat posed by the mages,' explained Shey.

'Tom might just be in special danger from the witches,' Alice told him. 'Helped to kill a Celtic witch back home, he did. Before she died, the witch threatened that the Morrigan would kill him if he ever dared to set foot on this island.'

'Probably just an empty threat,' said Shey. 'Most of the time the Morrigan sleeps – she only awakens and enters our world when summoned by a witch. This happens only rarely, for she is a difficult goddess to deal with and often vents her wrath on her own servants. So don't concern yourself unduly about it, boy. It's the mages who pose the greatest threat to us. And tomorrow, as we press on into Kerry, that threat will increase.'

Shey brought a map across to the table, unfolded it and spread it out. 'That's where we're bound for,' he said, jabbing his finger at the heart of the map. 'That's my home. I call it God's Country!'

It was a good name for a place you liked – but it was full of evil mages who practised dark magic and, no doubt, more than one Celtic witch. I studied the map and committed as much of it to memory as I could. In the work of a spook, you never know when knowledge of the terrain might come in useful.

CHAPTER 4
THE MIRROR

That night I had another lucid dream, reliving a scary incident from my past – the final encounter with the Celtic witch that Bill Arkwright and I had faced back home in the County.

I could see the witch just ahead of me now, running through the trees in the dappled moonlight. I was chasing her, closing fast, readying my silver chain, feeling confident that I could bind her. But I was about to cast it when she swerved away so that a tree stood between me and my target. Suddenly the burly figure of Bill Arkwright rose up to confront her and they collided. He fell, yet she only staggered for a second, then continued faster than ever.

We were now in the open, beyond the trees, sprinting towards a grassy burial mound. But just as I was about to throw my silver chain, a brilliant light blazed straight into my face, temporarily blinding me. Briefly the witch's silhouette stood out against a round yellow doorway. Then, suddenly, there was darkness and silence.

I came to a sharp halt, gasping for breath, taking stock of my surroundings. The air was warmer now, and absolutely still. Inside, beyond the doorway, lights flared on the rocky walls – black witch-candles. I could also see a small table and two wooden chairs.

To my dismay, I realized that I was now inside the burial mound! I'd followed the witch through the magical door she'd opened – and there she was, standing before me, an expression of wrath on her face. I took a few deep breaths to calm myself and slow my pounding heart.

'What a fool you be to follow me!' she cried.

'Do you always talk in rhyme?' I asked, trying to throw her off her guard.

It worked, and the witch didn't get a chance to reply because as I spoke I cast my silver chain; it brought her to her knees, the links stretched tight across her mouth to silence her. It was a perfect shot. I'd bound the witch, but now I had a real problem. I could no longer see a door. How was I going to get out of the mound?

Perhaps I'd be trapped inside it for ever. Never being able to wake up . . . It was a terrifying thought.

I searched the inside of the chamber carefully, running my fingers over the place where I seemed to have entered. But the rock was seamless. I was in a cave with no entrance. Arkwright was still on the outside; I really was trapped inside. Had I bound the witch or had *she* bound *me*?

I knelt close to her, staring into her eyes, which seemed to crinkle with amusement. Beneath the chain, her mouth was pulled away from her teeth; half a smile, half a grimace.

I urgently needed to find out how to leave the place. I needed to remove the chain from the witch's mouth so that she could speak.

But I didn't want to do it because I suddenly remembered what happened next.

The conscious part of me – the bit that knew I was having a dream – desperately fought for control. Somehow I knew I shouldn't be doing this. But I couldn't help myself. I was a prisoner of the dream, forced to follow that same risky course of action. So I eased the chain from her mouth. Now I had to face the consequences.

Her lips free of the chain, the witch was able to cast dark magic spells, and she started immediately. Speaking in the Old Tongue, she uttered three rapid phrases, each ending in a rhyme. Then she opened her mouth very wide, and a thick black cloud of smoke erupted from it.

I sprang to my feet and staggered backwards as the threatening cloud continued to grow. The witch's face was slowly being eclipsed, the cloud becoming denser and taking on an evil dark shape.

I could now see black-feathered wings, outstretched claws and a sharp beak. The cloud had turned into a black crow. The witch's open mouth was a portal to the dark! She had summoned her goddess, the Morrigan!

But this was not a bird of normal size and proportions; it was immense, distorted and twisted into something grotesque and evil. The beak, legs and claws were elongated, stretched out, reaching towards me, while the head and body remained at a distance, looking relatively small.

But then the wings grew too, until they reached out on either side of that monstrous bird to fill all the space available. They fluttered, battering wildly against the walls of the chamber, smashing the table so that it broke in half. The claws struck out at me. I ducked, and they raked against the wall above my head, gouging into the solid rock.

I was going to die here! But suddenly I was filled with inner strength. Confidence replaced fear; there was anger too.

I acted without conscious decision, and with a speed that astonished even me. I stepped forward, closer to the Morrigan, released my staff's retractable blade and swept it across from left to right. The blade cut deep into the bird's breast, slicing a bloody red line through the black feathers.

There was a blood-curdling scream. The goddess convulsed and contracted, shrinking rapidly until she was no larger than my fist. Then she vanished – though black feathers smeared with blood fluttered slowly to the ground.

Now I could once more see the witch: she shook her head, her expression one of acute astonishment. 'That's not possible!' she cried. 'Who are you that you can do such a thing?'

'My name's Tom Ward,' I told her. 'I'm a spook's apprentice and my job is to fight the dark.'

She smiled grimly. 'Well, you've fought your last battle, boy. There is no way you can escape this place, and soon the goddess will return. You will not find it so easy the second time.'

I smiled and glanced down at the blood-splattered feathers that littered the floor. Then I looked her straight in the eye, doing my best not to blink.

'We'll see. Next time I might cut off her head . . .'

I was bluffing, of course. I was just trying to appear more confident than I felt. I had to persuade this witch to open the door of the mound.

'Don't ever visit my land, boy!' she warned me. 'The Morrigan is much more powerful there. And she is vengeful. She would torment you beyond anything you can imagine. Whatever you do, stay away from Ireland!'

I awoke in a cold sweat, my heart pounding, relieved to see that it was almost dawn.

I remembered the dark days we'd spent on the Isle of Mona, struggling to survive. Then it was the Spook who had been plagued by nightmares. Mercifully, his had gone, but I seemed to have inherited them. Now I rarely enjoyed a restful dreamless sleep.

I went over in my mind what had actually happened next, back in the County. I'd made a bargain with the witch. In return for her opening the magical door, I'd promised she could go free as long as she left the

County and returned to Ireland. But once outside, I'd no sooner released her from my silver chain than Bill Arkwright had thrown his knife into her back, killing her on the spot. Later he'd cut out her heart and it had been eaten by his dogs – thus ensuring that she could not return from the dead.

So there was no way the same witch could be here in Ireland seeking revenge. I tried to convince myself of that, but I still felt uneasy and had a strong sense of foreboding – as if something had followed me back from the nightmare and was in the room with me.

Suddenly, from the far corner of the room, just by the door, I heard a faint noise. Could it be a mouse or a rat?

I listened carefully, but there was nothing. Maybe I'd been mistaken . . . Then it came again. This time it was like a footstep, and it was accompanied by another sound – one that filled me with new terror.

It was the sizzle and hiss of burning wood.

That sound brought back the memory of one of my worst experiences since becoming the Spook's apprentice. It usually heralded the approach of the

Fiend, his cloven hooves burning into the floorboards.

My heart lurched up into my mouth as I heard the terrifying sounds twice more in quick succession. I could now actually smell the burning wood!

But just when I thought the Fiend would appear by my side at any second, the sizzling ceased and the burning smell faded away. Then there was silence. I waited a long time before I dared to get out of bed. At last, summoning my courage, I got up, carrying my candle across to examine the floorboards. The last time I'd seen the Fiend manifest himself in this way, deep grooves had been burned into the floor. Here the prints had left only faint marks on the wood. But they were unmistakable: four cloven hoof prints leading from the door towards the bed.

Trying not to wake the household, I went to fetch my master and Alice and brought them to my room. My master shook his head; Alice looked really scared.

'There's little doubt, lad,' the Spook said. 'It's the Fiend for sure. I thought that jar was supposed to keep him at bay . . .'

'Let me see it again, Tom,' Alice demanded, holding out her hand.

'I fell on the jar when we faced that first jibber,' I told my master, handing it over. 'But I showed Alice and she thought it was all right.'

'Ain't sure that it's all right now,' she said, shaking her head and looking worried.

She carefully traced her finger along the line of the crack. When she held it up, there was a very faint red smear on it. 'It's hardly leaking at all – but there were only six drops of blood in the jar to start with. Its power to keep the Fiend at bay is slowly lessening. Time is running out for us . . .'

She didn't need to finish her sentence. As the jar's power weakened, the Fiend would be able to get closer and closer. Eventually he'd snatch me away into the dark – and destroy Alice too in revenge for the help she'd given me.

'We thought we had plenty of time to deal with the Fiend,' I said to my master. 'Now it's becoming urgent. The jar could fail at any moment.' I turned to Alice.

'Why don't you try and contact Grimalkin again?'

'I'll do my best, Tom. Just hope nothing's happened to her.'

The Spook said nothing, but his expression was grim. From his point of view it was all bad. By depending on the blood jar, we were already in collusion with the dark. If we didn't summon Grimalkin, the jar would eventually fail and the Fiend would come for me and Alice – the Spook too if he tried to get in the way. But in asking for Grimalkin's help, we were using the dark once again. I knew he felt trapped and compromised by the situation – and it was of my making.

The night had been cold and windless, and a heavy hoar frost whitened the ground as we set off west for Kerry. The early morning sun glittered off the still-distant snow-clad peaks ahead. Yet again Alice had failed to contact Grimalkin. She had been using a mirror, but in spite of her best efforts the witch assassin hadn't responded.

'I'll keep trying, Tom,' she told me. 'That's all I can

do. But I'm scared. There's no knowing how long we have before the jar fails.'

The Spook just shook his head and stared out of the window, watching the dogs as they ran alongside the carriage. There was nothing to be said. Nothing we could do. If Grimalkin didn't answer soon, it would all be over. Death and an eternity of torment awaited us.

Within the hour, a group of armed riders in emerald-green tunics joined us to provide an escort – two ahead of our carriage, four behind. All day we continued southwest, our elevation increasing as the brooding mountains ahead reared up into the cloudless pale blue sky. Then, as the sun began to sink towards the west, we saw the sea below us, and a small town huddled on the edge of a river estuary.

'That's Kenmare, my home town,' said Shey. 'It's a haven from the mages. They have never attacked us here – at least not yet. My house lies on the edge of a wood to the west.'

The house proved to be an elegant mansion built in

the shape of a letter E; the three wings were each three storeys high. The doors were stout and the windows on the ground floor were shuttered. Additionally there was a high wall completely encircling it. Entry to the grounds was through a single wrought-iron gate, which was just wide enough to allow our carriage to pass. It certainly provided a good deal of protection from attack. There were also armed guards patrolling both the inside and outside of the wall.

The hospitality of our host was excellent and we dined well that night.

'What do you think of this green country of ours?' he asked.

'It's like home,' I told him. 'It reminds me of the County where we live.'

His face broke into a grin. I had said the right thing, but in truth mine was an honest reply. I had meant every word.

'It's a troubled land with a proud but good-hearted people,' he said. 'But the Otherworld is never very far away.'

'The Otherworld?' asked the Spook. 'What do you mean by that?'

'It's the place where the dead heroes of Ireland dwell, awaiting their chance to be reborn.'

The Spook nodded, but was too polite to air his true thoughts. After all, we were guests, and our host had been generous indeed. By the 'Otherworld', Farrell Shey probably meant the dark. I knew nothing about Irish heroes, but it was certainly true that some malevolent witches had returned from the dark to be born again into this world.

'We don't have many heroes in the County, alive or dead,' Alice said, grinning mischievously. 'All we have are spooks and their daft apprentices!'

The Spook frowned at Alice but I just smiled. I knew she didn't mean it.

My master turned to Farrell Shey and asked, 'Would you tell us something of your Irish heroes? We're strangers to your land and would like to know more about it.'

Shey smiled. 'Were I to give you a full account of

Ireland's heroes, we'd be here for days, so I'll just tell you briefly about the greatest of them all. His name is Cuchulain, also known as the Hound of Calann. He was given that second name because, when he was a young man, he fought a huge, fierce hound with his bare hands. He killed it by dashing its brains out against a gatepost.

'He was immensely strong and skilled with sword and spear, but he is most famed for his battle frenzy – a kind of berserker fury. His muscles and his whole body would swell; one eye would recede back into his skull while the other bulged from his massive forehead. Some say that, in battle, blood erupted from every pore of his body; others that it was merely the blood of the enemies he slew. He defended his homeland many times, winning great victories against terrible odds. But he died young.'

'How did he meet his end?' asked the Spook.

'He was cursed by witches,' Shey replied. 'They withered his left shoulder and arm so that his strength was diminished by half. Even so, he continued to fight and took the lives of many of his enemies. His end came when the Morrigan, the goddess of slaughter, turned against him. She had loved him but he had rejected her advances. In revenge she used her powers against him. Weakened, he suffered a mortal wound to the stomach, and his enemies cut off his head. Now he waits in the Otherworld until it is time for him to return and save Ireland again.'

We ate in silence for a while: Shey was clearly saddened by the memory of Cuchulain's death, while the Spook seemed deep in thought. For my part I had been unsettled by that mention of the Morrigan. I met Alice's eyes and saw that her mischievous teasing had been replaced by fear. She was thinking of the threat to me.

'I'm intrigued by your talk of this "Otherworld",' said the Spook, breaking the silence. 'I know that your witches can use magical doors to enter ancient burial mounds. Can they also enter the Otherworld?'

'They can – and often do so,' said Shey. 'In fact, another name for the Otherworld is the Hollow Hills.

73

Those mounds are actually gateways to that domain. But even witches don't stay there long. It is a dangerous place, but within it there are places of refuge. They are called *sidhes* and, although to ordinary human eyes they look like churches, they are actually forts that can withstand even an assault by a god. But a sidhe is a dwelling for a hero: only the worthy can enter. A lesser being would be destroyed in an instant – both body and soul extinguished.'

His words brought back an image from my recurrent nightmare. Running from the Morrigan, I'd sought refuge in what appeared to be a church. Was it really a sidhe? My dreams were starting to make some kind of sense to me. Was I learning from them, gaining knowledge that might help me in the future? I wondered.

'You see, that's what the mages ultimately seek,' continued Shey. 'By drawing enough strength from Pan, they hope one day to gain control of the Otherworld – which contains items that could endow them with immense power back here.'

'What things?' asked the Spook. 'Spells? Dark magical power?'

'Could be,' said Shey. 'But also weapons of great potency manufactured by the gods themselves. Some believe that a war-hammer forged by the blacksmith god, Hephaestus, is hidden there. Once thrown, it never misses its target and always returns to its owner's hand. Doolan, the Butcher, would love to get his hands on something like that!'

The Spook thanked our host for the information, and the topic of conversation changed to farming and hopes for the next potato crop. There had been two bad years of blight: another poor harvest would bring many people close to starvation. I began to feel guilty. We had dined well during our stay in Ireland while, out there, people were going hungry.

We were all tired after the journey and went to bed early. Alice was in the next room, close enough to be protected by the blood jar, the Spook further down the corridor. I was just about to undress and climb into bed when I heard a muffled voice.

I opened the door and peered out. There was nobody there. I stepped through the doorway, heard the voice again, and realized that it was coming from Alice's room. Who was she talking to? I leaned against her door and listened. It was definitely Alice's voice, but hers alone. She seemed to be chanting rather than engaged in conversation with someone else.

I eased open her door and crept in, closing it carefully behind me so as not to make a noise. Alice was seated in front of the dressing-table mirror, gazing into it intently. By her side stood a candle.

Suddenly she stopped chanting and I saw that she was mouthing something silently into the mirror. Some witches wrote on mirrors, but the more skilled used lip-reading. She must be trying to reach Grimalkin.

My heart leaped, for instead of Alice's reflection I could see the outline of a woman's head in the mirror. From my position by the door I couldn't make out her features, but for a moment my blood ran cold.

However, as I moved closer to this mirror, the chill quickly passed, for now I recognized Grimalkin's face.

Alice had established contact at last. I was elated, filled with hope. Perhaps the witch assassin would soon come to Ireland and help us to bind the Fiend so that we could finally stop relying on the failing blood jar.

I knew that if she emerged from her trance and found me sitting there, she might get a terrible shock, so I left, shutting the door quietly behind me. Once back in my room, I sat down on the chair and waited for her. I felt certain that she'd soon come and tell me about her conversation with Grimalkin.

The next thing I knew, I was sitting up with a jolt. I'd fallen asleep. It was the middle of the night and my candle had burned low. I was surprised to find that Alice hadn't paid me a visit, but maybe she'd fallen asleep too. We'd been travelling for two days and were both tired. So I got undressed and climbed into bed.

A gentle rap on my door awoke me. I sat up. The

morning sun was streaming through the curtains. The door opened slightly and I saw that Alice was standing there, smiling at me.

'Still in bed, sleepy head?' she said. 'We're already late for breakfast. I can hear them talking. Can't you smell the bacon?'

I smiled back. 'See you downstairs!' I said.

It was only when Alice had left and I started to get dressed that I realized she hadn't mentioned talking to Grimalkin in the mirror. I frowned. Surely it was too important to leave until later, I thought.

For a moment I considered the possibility that I'd just dreamed it, but my master had always stressed the importance of knowing the difference between waking and dreaming. The state in between could sometimes be a problem for spooks; that was when witches and other servants of the dark sometimes tried to influence you for their own ends. It was vital to know which was which. No – I knew it hadn't been a dream.

I went down to breakfast and was soon tucking into pork sausages and bacon while my master questioned our host further about our enemies, the goat mages.

I was only half listening to what was being said. I wanted to get Alice alone as soon as possible so that I could ask her about last night. Was Grimalkin finally on her way to join us? Would she reach us before the protection of the blood jar failed? Why hadn't Alice mentioned her conversation to the Spook as well? There was something strange and worrying going on here.

'I need a bit of air – I'm going for a walk,' I said, getting to my feet. 'The dogs could do with some exercise, anyway.'

'I'll come with you,' Alice said with a smile. Of course, that's what I'd planned: she couldn't afford to be separated from the blood jar.

'It would be best not to wander too far from the house,' said Shey. 'Kenmare is a refuge, but even though I have guards watching the approaches to the town, the area is not entirely safe. Our enemies will almost certainly be watching us.'

'Aye, lad. Take heed,' added the Spook. 'We're in a

land that's strange to us and we're dealing with the unknown.'

With a nod of agreement, I left the dining room with Alice. We went to the kennels to collect Claw, Blood and Bone, and were soon passing through the front gate and striding briskly down the slope away from the house. It was a fine sunny morning again, the very best that could be hoped for in late winter, and the dogs raced ahead excitedly, following scents and barking loudly.

Keeping an eye out for anything untoward, we entered a small wood where the ground was still white with frost, and there I paused beneath the bare branches of a sycamore and came directly to the point.

'I heard you chanting at the mirror last night, Alice. I went into your room and saw you talking to Grimalkin. What did she say? Is she on her way? I'm surprised you haven't told me about it already . . .' I tried to keep the annoyance out of my voice.

Alice looked flustered for a moment and bit her lip. 'Sorry, Tom,' she said. 'Was going to tell you but thought it best to wait a while. It ain't good news.'

'What? You mean she isn't able to join us?'

'She's coming, all right, but it could be some time before she manages it. Enemy soldiers swept through Pendle and tried to clear out the witch clans. At first it went their way, and they burned some houses and killed a few witches. But once it was dark, the clans conjured up a thick fog and, after scaring the men, drove them into Witch Dell, where many met their deaths. The witches feasted well that night. Though that didn't satisfy the Malkins, because they sent Grimalkin after the commander, who had taken refuge in Caster Castle.

'Grimalkin scaled the walls at midnight and killed him in his bed. She took his thumb-bones and wrote a curse on the bedroom wall in his blood.'

I shivered at that. The witch assassin was ruthless and could be cruel when the situation demanded it. Nobody would want to be on the wrong side of her.

'After that there was a price on her head, and every enemy soldier north of Priestown is hunting her down,' Alice continued. 'She's hoping to reach Scotland

and get a boat from there to bring her to Ireland.'

'I still don't know why you didn't tell me this earlier.'

'Sorry, Tom, but I really did think it was best to keep the bad news from you for a while.'

'But it's not that *bad*, Alice. Grimalkin escaped and, although delayed, is still on her way.'

Alice lowered her eyes and looked down at her pointy shoes. 'There's more, Tom . . . I can't hide anything from you for long, can I? You see, Grimalkin's worried about you. She wants to destroy the Fiend, she does, but believes that she can only do it with your help. She believes what your mam said – that you will find a way to finish him. But now she's been warned by a scryer that you're in danger – that you risk death at the hands of a dead witch . . .'

'What – you mean—?'

'Yes – the Celtic witch you mentioned – the one Old Arkwright killed. Grimalkin said she's back from the dead and she's hunting you down.'

Images from my nightmare came vividly into my mind. Were they a warning? Perhaps that's why I kept having the same dream over and over again. But how could *that* witch be after me? I wondered.

'It's not possible, Alice. She can't come back. Bill Arkwright fed her heart to his dogs!'

'Are you sure? Grimalkin seemed certain that she was right,' Alice said.

'I was there when he did it, Alice. I saw him throw it to Claw and her pups.'

If you hanged a witch, she could come back from the dead, but there were two ways to make sure that she couldn't return. One was to burn her; the other was to cut out her heart and eat it. This was why Bill Arkwright always fed the hearts of water witches to his dogs. He'd done the same with the Celtic witch: it was a tried and tested spook's method – it *always* worked. That witch was dead beyond any hope of return.

'Do you remember me telling you about my dream, Alice – the one about the Morrigan?' I asked her.

She nodded.

'Well, I've been having that same nightmare every night. A large black crow is flying after me. I'm in a forest, running towards a chapel. It's my only chance of refuge and I have to get inside before midnight – otherwise it'll be the end of me. But then the crow shifts its shape. It's standing nearby, with the body of a woman but the head of a crow . . .'

'Ain't no doubt about it – that's the Morrigan for sure,' said Alice.

'But then the crow's head slowly changes into a human one. And I've seen that face before. It's the witch that Bill Arkwright killed. But why should the Morrigan take on the dead witch's face?'

'Maybe she wants vengeance for what you and Bill Arkwright did,' suggested Alice. 'Using her dead servant's face is a way of warning you what's going to happen. Don't like to say this, Tom, but it could be more than just an ordinary nightmare.'

I nodded. Scary as it was, that seemed likely. It could be a direct warning from the Morrigan, one of the most vengeful and bloodthirsty of the Old Gods.

My sense of foreboding was growing. Not only did we face the approaching goat-mage rituals, but now the threat from the Morrigan seemed imminent too. It was a relief to know that Grimalkin would soon be joining us – though that would bring another challenge: the attempt to bind the Fiend. We might soon have three powerful entities from the dark to contend with all at once.

I reached into my pocket and pulled out the blood jar, holding it up to the light and examining it carefully. Was the crack a little bigger? It certainly seemed to be. I handed it to Alice.

'Is the damage worse?' I asked her nervously.

Alice studied the jar for a long time, turning it over and over in her hands. Then she handed it back to me. 'The crack could be lengthening a bit,' she admitted, 'but it's not leaking any more blood. Don't worry, Tom. When Grimalkin arrives, we can bind the Fiend and we won't need that jar any more.'

We walked slowly back to the house, the dogs following at our heels. By now clouds had blown in from the west to obscure the sun. It looked like the period of good settled weather was over. I could smell rain.

CHAPTER 5
KILLORGLIN

When we returned to Farrell Shey's house, the Spook was pacing back and forth outside the gate. He had a worried look on his face.

'Where have you been?' he demanded. 'I expected you back an hour ago. Weren't you warned not to go too far from the house? I thought something had happened to you.'

'But we haven't been very far away,' I protested. 'We've just been talking, that's all. Alice has made contact with Grimalkin. She is on her way here at last. It could take her a while, but she's coming. So that's good news, isn't it?'

Of course, I didn't tell the Spook everything. He'd

find it hard enough to work with the witch assassin without knowing the details of what she'd done to the enemy commander.

'Aye, lad, it certainly is.' He looked a little more cheerful now. 'But while you've been away, things have been decided. As a matter of fact, they were being decided at the breakfast table, but you seemed to have other matters on your mind. In a couple of years you'll have finished your training and you'll be a spook yourself. It's time to think and behave like a spook. You should have been concentrating, not away with the fairies.'

'I'm sorry,' I said, hanging my head. I could tell he was disappointed in me. 'So what's happening then?'

'Up until now the landowners have attacked the mages just before the goat ritual,' my master explained; 'usually as they left the fort and travelled to Killorglin. But this time it will be different. Farrell Shey thinks it'll be about a week before most of the mages travel to the town, but they always send a few men on in advance to secure their accommodation and build the tower for the platform they use in the ritual. He's going to hide some of his men in Killorglin to take the advance party by surprise, and we're going with them. You see, we need to try and capture one of the goat mages and question him. It might be possible to learn some of the secrets of the ceremony – maybe even how to halt or counter it.

'Of course, the hard part will be reaching Killorglin without the mages' spies warning them of our presence. So Shey's summoning scores of armed men. They'll spend the day scouring the surrounding countryside and clearing it of danger.'

'But with all that activity, won't the mages guess that something is up?' I asked.

'Aye, lad, they might – but they won't know exactly what. It's far better than allowing their spies to report back to the Staigue on our departure from the house and the direction we take.'

The Land Alliance men returned at dusk, declaring the whole area to be safe. So, leaving the dogs and our bags behind, the Spook, Alice and I set off for Killorglin under cover of darkness, in the company of about a dozen burly men under Shey's command.

We travelled on foot, through the mountains, following a slow arc as we climbed northeast, a heavy cold drizzle slowly turning the trail to mud. As dawn approached, we skirted the shore of a large lake before reaching the small town of Killarney. We took refuge in a barn on the outskirts, and slept through the daylight hours before setting off again.

By now the rain had stopped and the going was easier. Soon we were following the banks of the mist-shrouded river Laune, and we arrived on the outskirts of Killorglin long before dawn. Making camp in a large muddy field on the edge of the town, we joined scores of others who had arrived in anticipation of the Puck Fair. Warming our hands by the fire, we asked Farrell Shey about the large numbers of people already gathering.

'I'm surprised to see so many here this early,' said the Spook. 'The fair itself is still several days away.'

In the grey dawn light the field was bustling with activity. Some had set up stalls and were selling food: strings of sausages, onions and carrots. There were a large number of animals too – horses were being galloped up and down the field, presenting a great risk to those on foot.

'These people don't seem to be starving,' I commented.

'There are always some who prosper, however bad things get,' Shey replied. 'Believe me, there are a lot of hungry mouths out there. Many folk will be too weak to walk to Killorglin. Despite that, the fair gets bigger every year. Winter or summer makes no difference: even in bad weather, hundreds are drawn here. They come from miles around. Many are traders who bring animals to sell or barter, but there are also tinkers and fortune-tellers, as well as thieves – particularly cutpurses. The town quickly becomes too full to accommodate them all. This field is just one of many that will eventually be filled to bursting.'

'What about the mages?' asked the Spook.

'They will have commandeered most of the accom-modation in the town – particularly overlooking the triangular market at its centre, where the platform is erected. For the duration of the main festival, Killorglin effectively belongs to them. But this time we'll give them a surprise!'

We entered the town late in the morning, jostling through the narrow streets towards its centre, where a market was being held. The stalls were packed tightly into the cobbled heart of Killorglin. Most small towns had a square or rectangular market area, but this was indeed triangular; it sloped away towards a lane that led down a steep hill to a distant river and bridge.

Shey had donned a rough woollen cloak to hide his fine clothes and nobody gave us a second glance. We mingled with the throng of people while he hired a room in what seemed to be the smallest and shabbiest of the many inns overlooking the busy market. We quickly appreciated that it was an excellent choice for, unlike the majority of the other inns, it was accessed from a street parallel to the western edge of the cobbled triangle, and we could enter and leave without being noticed by anyone in the marketplace.

'This is the last inn the mages are likely to choose,' Shey said, smoothing back his white hair. 'They like their comfort and are also protective of their status – only the very best for them. If it's been booked at all, this place will only be used by their servants.'

We returned to the field, where Shey's men were cooking over a fire. However, before the sun went down, word reached us that a small group of mages had travelled through the mountain passes north of the Staigue ring fort and, walking through the night, were heading directly towards Killorglin. They would be here before dawn. We'd arrived just in time.

Taking some provisions for our vigil, we went back to the room overlooking the marketplace, from where we could watch for the arrival of our enemies. We drew the curtains across the window, leaving a small gap in the centre. The sky was cloudless, and a moon that had waned three days beyond the full cast down a silver light onto the empty streets.

About two hours before dawn we heard the *clip-clop* of hooves. Two riders came into view, followed by four men carrying large bundles over their shoulders.

'The mages are the ones on horseback,' Shey explained. 'The others are workmen who'll construct the platform.'

Both horses were thoroughbreds, black stallions designed for speed, and their riders were armed with large curved swords that broadened as they reached the point – the ones known as scimitars. The mages dismounted and made for the highest point of the cobbled triangle. They were tall, powerfully built men with dark bushy eyebrows and short pointy beards known as goatees; so called because they mimic the tuft of hair on the chin of a goat.

They pointed down at the cobbles and, without further delay, the four carpenters set about erecting the tall wooden structure that would house the platform. Their bundles consisted of tools and what looked like specially crafted pieces of wood. A pair of the men soon went off and returned after a few minutes with two large wooden beams. These must have been produced locally, ready to meet their needs. No sooner had they laid them down beside their tools than they set off again, returning with more wood. Soon the sounds of hammering and banging disturbed the peace of the night, and the tower slowly began to take shape.

All through that day the carpenters worked, while the mages squatted on the ground or prowled around the growing tower, issuing instructions.

The people of Killorglin stayed away from the marketplace, and that day no stalls were set up.

'Are they scared of the mages?' I asked. 'Is that why there's no market today?'

'They're scared, all right,' Shey answered. 'During the construction of the platform, they usually give the area a wide berth. But once the goat is in position, they come back, and the market is busier than ever – though mostly with those buying pots of ale and bottles of wine. Many people get drunk – perhaps to escape the horrors the mages bring to their town. For others it's one of the two highlights of the year, and everything is taken to excess.'

'When do you plan to try and snatch one of the mages?' asked the Spook.

'At dusk,' Shey answered. 'We'll burn the wooden tower too. No doubt they'll rebuild it, but that'll mean bringing fresh materials from Staigue. It'll set their preparations back a little at least.'

'Will they use dark magic to defend themselves?' my master wondered.

'They may try,' said Shey, 'but' – he gazed at us steadfastly – 'I have faith in our combined strength. I'm confident of success.'

'Well, I have my silver chain,' said the Spook. 'The boy too. That'll bind him more securely than any rope.'

A silver chain worked against witches and most mages. It seemed straightforward: we outnumbered the two mages and their workmen, and would have the element of surprise. But then, out of the corner of my eye, I noticed Alice's expression. She looked worried.

'What's wrong, Alice?' I asked.

'Ain't binding the mage that bothers me,' she said. 'It's afterwards, when the others find out what's been done. They'll come after us – and there's lots of them.'

'That's all been thought through and carefully planned, girl,' the Spook told her. 'The captured horses and any other prisoners will be taken southeast, back the way we came. But the four of us, with our special prisoner, are going in another direction – down the coast. There's a castle there – Ballycarbery, the home of another of the landowners; it's a strong fortress, where we can question the captive mage in safety.'

The sun went down and, as the light began to fail, it was time for us to act.

Below us, the structure was almost completed: a tall square wooden shaft balanced on the cobbles; at over thirty feet high, it now dominated the market area. It was a remarkable achievement for just one day's work. The exhausted workmen were packing up their tools while the two mages waited patiently with folded arms, their horses tethered to a post at the far corner. Our men had reported that they had taken rooms in the largest of the inns facing us, and would soon retire there for the night.

We left our vantage point, went downstairs into the street and headed for the edge of the market area, taking care to keep to the shadows. With the Spook and Shey in the lead, we began a slow, stealthy approach, knowing that our armed forces were moving in from behind, cutting off any chance of escape.

Suddenly the tethered horses reared up and whinnied nervously. They must have caught our scent and, instantly alerted, the two mages drew their scimitars and took up a defensive position, back to back. Shey and my master left the shadows and began to charge towards our enemies, with Alice and me close behind them. I could hear shouts of command and other footsteps running through the darkness as our force converged on its target.

The nearest mage raised his weapon, but the Spook

cast his silver chain as he ran. With a mighty crack, it soared aloft to form a perfect spiral. It was a good, accurate throw and it dropped over the head and shoulders of the mage, pinning his arms to his sides so that his sword fell to the cobbles with a clatter. So excellent a shot was it that part of the chain tightened about his eyes and mouth so that he could neither see nor speak. Binding the mouth was very important when dealing with a witch capable of uttering dark magical spells. Mages used spells too, so my master had taken no chances.

The other mage whirled round to meet Shey, and there was a metallic rasp as their two blades came together hard. Then the mage cried out, dropped his scimitar and fell hard onto his face; he lay there twitching as the blood started to pool beneath him. The four workmen dropped to their knees with their hands raised above their heads, begging for their lives. Shey's men were encircling us now, and it was but the work of minutes to bind the carpenters with ropes and lead them and the two horses away.

So while our men prepared to travel southeast towards Killarney, the Spook, Shey, Alice and I took our prisoner in the direction of Ballycarbery Castle near the small town of Cahersiveen.

Once on the road and clear of Killorglin, I glanced back and saw dark smoke and a red glow over the rooftops. Shey's men were burning the wooden platform; the efforts of the workmen had been in vain. It had gone well, but I couldn't help but worry that the fire would act like a beacon, drawing our enemies towards the town in force.

CHAPTER 6
AN INSTRUMENT OF TORTURE

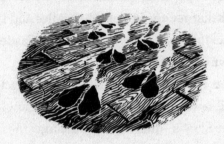

Ballycarbery appeared to be a strong fortress, with thick stone walls and only one gate which faced west. However, the castle didn't have a moat with a drawbridge and, from my own experience of such fortifications, it seemed to me that this was a major weakness. It meant that an enemy could approach right up to the ramparts. As a fortress, it had seen better days. Its walls were also overgrown with ivy. Determined attackers could use that to scale the walls.

Still bound with the Spook's silver chain, the mage was taken down to the dungeons to await interrogation in the morning. We were given comfortable beds in the castle, and wasted no time in settling down to catch up on our sleep. Checking the blood jar before I dozed off, I couldn't help reflecting that in the past our situation had often been very different. In such fortifications as this we had languished in dark, damp dungeons awaiting death while our enemies had been in a position of power.

I dreamed again – the same nightmare in which I was being pursued by the Morrigan in the shape of a crow. But it seemed to me that this dream was slightly less scary than the previous one. The goddess was still gradually drawing nearer, but I was running faster, getting closer and closer to the unseen refuge.

I suddenly awoke in a cold sweat, my heart hammering, but I felt somewhat encouraged. Was I learning; getting slightly stronger each time I experienced the nightmare?

At that moment something happened that was more frightening than any night terror.

I heard the dull *thud*, *thud*, *thud* of footsteps approaching my bed, accompanied by the sizzle of burning wood. I tried to open my eyes but my eyelids were too heavy; my breath came in ragged gasps, my heart beating painfully in my chest. I sensed something huge close to the bed; something reaching towards me. Then I felt hot breath on my face, smelled the fetid stink. And a voice I knew only too well spoke right beside my left ear. It was the Fiend:

'You're almost mine now, Tom. I can nearly reach you. Just a little while longer and the jar will fail! Then you'll be mine!'

I opened my eyes, expecting to see his huge head with its curved horns and mouthful of sharp teeth. But to my relief there was nothing. I scrambled out of bed, and soon realized that it had been more than a dream: here too a set of hoof prints had been burned into the floorboards. They were scorched deeper than on the last occasion in my room at the inn. Time was running out. The power of the blood jar was almost at an end.

I didn't tell either Alice or the Spook what had happened. Why add to their fears? It was something that we could do nothing about. I just had to hope that Grimalkin would arrive soon.

After breakfast we walked down to the dungeons with Shey and three armed guards to begin questioning the prisoner.

'He's had neither food nor water,' Shey remarked as we approached the cell door. 'That should loosen his tongue a little.'

Two of the guards joined us inside the cold damp cell while the other locked us in with the mage and stood guard outside. No chances were being taken, and the powers of our enemy were certainly not being underestimated.

The cell was spacious and clearly designed for the interrogation of prisoners. Although there was no place to sleep, other than a pallet of straw in a corner, it contained a table and three chairs, one with leather straps to confine a captive. Deftly the Spook uncoiled his silver chain from the mage, who was quickly gagged and then had his arms tied behind his back. Finally he was strapped into the chair, and the Spook and they seated themselves, facing him across the table.

There was a candle on the table and a torch in a wall bracket beside the door, providing ample light for what we needed. There was also a large jug of water and two small cups. Alice and I stood behind the Spook and Shey, while the two guards positioned themselves close to the prisoner's chair.

'We are going to ask you a few questions,' Shey said, his breath steaming in the candlelight. 'You would be wise to answer truthfully. Failure to do so will lead to dire consequences. Do you understand?'

The mage nodded. At a sign from Shey, a guard pulled the gag from his mouth. Immediately the prisoner began to choke and cough; he seemed to be struggling for words.

'Water – give me water, please!' he begged at last, his voice hoarse.

'You'll get water in a while,' Shey told him. 'But first you must answer our questions!' Then he turned to the Spook and nodded.

'Why does the goat ceremony sometimes fail?' my master asked without delay.

'I will tell you nothing!' the mage replied with a scowl. 'Nothing at all!'

'We'll get it out of you one way or the other,' said Shey. 'There's a hard way or an easy way. You choose . . .'

'Whether I live or die here is of no concern to me.'

'Then you're either a brave man or a fool!' snapped Shey. 'No doubt the latter,' he added, reaching into his pocket and pulling out a small metal implement, which he placed on the table before the mage. It looked like a pair of tongs. 'There will be pain before you die. Terrible pain! Is that what you want?'

The Spook scowled and his eyes flashed. 'Just what do you mean by that?' he demanded of Shey, pointing down at the implement.

Farrell Shey picked up the tool, which I now saw was more like blacksmith's pliers. 'This is a versatile instrument,' he said quietly, 'which can be used in various ways to persuade a reluctant prisoner to talk. It can crush fingers or extract teeth.'

'I don't hold with torture!' The Spook's voice was angry. 'And only a fool uses it. Subject someone to pain and they will say anything just to bring it to an end. Many who are falsely accused of witchcraft confess under torture. The temporary relief from the pain is soon followed by the greater pain of execution and death. So put away that implement or I'll continue with this no longer!'

I felt proud to be a spook. We were honourable in the way we went about our work.

Shey scowled and pursed his lips in anger, but nevertheless he returned the instrument of torture to his pocket. No doubt the long years of strife between the mages and the landowners had caused great bitterness, with atrocities committed by both sides. The dark was growing in power and it corrupted even those who opposed it. I had compromised myself, using the dark in order to survive, so I was in no position to judge anyone.

My master then repeated his question: 'The goat ceremony – why does it sometimes fail?'

The mage hesitated, but then fixed his eyes on the Spook and muttered, 'It is because what we do is not pleasing to our god.'

'But don't you *know* what pleases him?' asked the Spook. 'You've been carrying out your dark rituals for centuries. Surely you must know by now?'

'It depends on many things. These are variables which cannot be predicted.'

'What variables?'

'I thirst. My throat is dry. Give me a little water and I will tell you . . .'

On impulse, and not waiting for Shey's response, I stepped forward, picked up the jug and poured a little water into the nearer of the two cups, then held it to the mage's lips and tilted it slightly. The man's Adam's apple wobbled as he gulped the water eagerly. Once he'd finished I spoke for the first time since entering the room.

'What's your name?' I asked.

'Cormac,' the mage replied.

Shey scowled at me, but the Spook smiled

107

and nodded as if he approved of my initiative.

'Now, Cormac,' he said. 'What are the variables?'

'The choice of goat is important. It becomes the sacred host which our god, Pan, must enter. He will not assume the body of one that is not pleasing to him. Seven goats are selected initially. Together we must choose the best. The process is not easy. Our seers debate our choice for days.'

My master nodded. 'What are the other variables?' he demanded.

'We must make human sacrifices – three in all. These also have to be perfect. One must be female, and she must choose to die, giving her life gladly. The other two must be mages who also freely offer their lives to the god. I am to be one of the sacrifices. The other died at *your* hands beside the wooden tower!' he said, glaring angrily at Shey.

The Spook nodded thoughtfully. 'So the two mages who volunteer to die are responsible for overseeing the construction of the platform?'

'Yes, it's an ancient custom.'

'So what will happen now that one of the volunteers is already dead?'

'His name was Mendace: he was a brave man whose death at the hands of our enemies is as acceptable to Pan as if it had been part of the ceremony. That did not harm our cause.'

'And what of you, Cormac?' asked my master. 'If you were to die here, then your death would be equally acceptable?'

'Yes – if you kill me, you will contribute directly to the ritual,' the mage said, smiling for the first time. 'That is why I am not afraid. I welcome death!'

'And if we choose not to kill you?'

Cormac didn't answer, and it was the Spook's turn to smile. 'Then once the process has begun, a substitute is not allowed? To ensure success it must be you and no other! So if we keep you safe on this occasion, the raising of Pan will probably fail . . .'

The mage lowered his gaze and stared at the table for a long time without speaking.

'I think Cormac's silence tells it all,' the Spook said at

last, turning towards Shey. 'We've already achieved our purpose. All we have to do now is keep him imprisoned here. Can this castle be defended against an attack by the mages?'

'No castle is completely impregnable,' answered Shey. 'And our enemies will be desperate – they might well move against us here.'

'Then you need to bring in as many men as possible to defend it, and also to stock it well against siege,' my master advised. 'Things couldn't be better. Hold out here, and then, in midsummer, before they can try again and are weaker than ever, move against Staigue directly and finish them once and for all – that's my advice.'

Shey smiled. 'It's good advice, John Gregory. We'll do just that. Centuries of strife could be over at last, ending with their defeat. I thank you.'

Alice had been a silent witness to the interrogation, but now she gave the prisoner a steely stare. 'Who's the woman – the one who volunteered herself for sacrifice?' she asked.

For a moment I thought he wasn't going to answer, but then he stared straight at her. 'It's a witch – one of those who ally themselves with us.'

Alice nodded and then exchanged a quick nervous glance with me. So one of the Celtic witches was in the area and would have gone to Killorglin to sacrifice herself. Now she would no doubt come here, joining the siege of Ballycarbery Castle.

CHAPTER 7
THE SIEGE OF BALLYCARBERY CASTLE

They sent messengers with word of the situation, and immediately preparations to defend the castle got underway. I was relieved to see a score of men begin to hack the ivy from the walls to prevent the enemy from climbing it.

The following day the landowners' men started to arrive. There were far fewer than I'd expected – no more than fifty in all – but each small group brought with them weapons and food and supplies in excess of their own needs so that the castle was now adequately stocked for the anticipated siege – although we probably had fewer than eighty men to call upon.

'I'd have thought you'd have been able to find more

to rally to your cause,' said the Spook as we gazed down from the western battlements on what the leader of the Land Alliance had told us would be the final contingent to arrive. It consisted of five armed men and two small wagons, each pulled by a donkey that seemed overburdened by the load and near to collapse.

'It's neither better nor worse than I'd hoped,' said Shey. 'Each landowner must also look to his own defences, and ensure that he has enough servants with him.'

The Spook nodded, pondering the answer while he gazed at the sun, which was sinking low towards the sea. 'When will they attack?' he asked.

'Tonight or tomorrow,' Shey replied. 'They will come east through the mountains.'

'How many?'

'Probably about a hundred and fifty, by our most recent estimate.'

'As many as that?' The Spook raised his eyebrows in surprise. 'How many of those will be mages?'

'In total there are probably about fifteen or so, along

with half a dozen who are being trained. Probably about two thirds of that number will come here. The rest will stay behind in their fort at Staigue.'

'And the others? Who are their servants and supporters?'

'They keep about thirty armed men, and perhaps another ten who work as cooks and craftsmen, such as butchers, tanners and masons. But they can draw on many more to swell their ranks when it comes to a battle. These conscripts are taken from among the poor – those with a only tiny cottage and very little land, who live on the edge of starvation. They fight alongside the mages in return for food for their families, but also out of fear. Who can refuse the call to arms when an emissary of the mages visits your lonely cottage and summons you? The people they recruit now will be poorly armed and often weakened by hunger.'

'And no doubt you and your servants will have eaten well through the winter; you'll be strong and better able to fight . . .' said the Spook.

I could hear the disapproval in my master's voice,

but Shey didn't seem to notice. I agreed with the Spook. We had to make a stand against the dark and the threat posed by the mages, but as was often the case in this world, the powerful fought for land or pride while poor folk suffered.

'That is certainly true,' Shey replied. 'We will have food and supplies inside the castle while the recruits outside will receive only meagre rations. I estimate that in less than a week, if they have not breached our walls, the mages will be forced to retire, defeated. We will harry them all the way back to their fort. And perhaps Staigue will finally fall, giving us victory at last.'

I slept well that night, but was brought out of a deep sleep by Alice shaking my arm. It was still dark outside and she was holding a candle.

'They're here, Tom!' she cried, her voice full of concern. 'The mages! And there are so many of them!'

I followed her to the window, which faced east, and gazed out. There were lights snaking towards us as far as the eye could see. Our enemies had certainly arrived in force. It was impossible to count them, but judging by the lights, more were here than Shey had predicted.

'Don't worry, Alice,' I said, trying to reassure her. 'We have enough food here to last for weeks, and anyway, once the time for the ceremony has passed, the siege will be in vain – they'll go away.'

We sat together by the window, holding hands but not speaking. Enemy campfires began to spark into life, encircling the castle completely. No doubt Alice was thinking the same thing as me: the Celtic witch would be down there, sitting by one of those fires. Was it the one seeking revenge? Would she know that I was here? I reassured myself with the thought that she couldn't reach me – the thick castle walls would keep her away.

But the dawn brought news to shatter some of my hopes. A team of oxen was slowly dragging something towards the castle – a big metal cylinder on wheels. They had a siege gun – a big eighteen-pounder!

Alice and I had both seen such a powerful gun in action. One had been used by soldiers to breach the walls of Malkin Tower. It had been fired with great accuracy, the huge cannonballs striking almost exactly the same spot in the wall, until at last it had given way and was open to the attackers. But a lot would depend on the skill of the gunners here. Would they be experienced enough to breach the defences of Ballycarbery Castle?

Neither Shey nor his men seemed much perturbed by what was happening outside our walls. After a hearty breakfast of oats and honey, Alice and I joined him and the Spook on the battlements.

'Did you know they'd have a siege gun?' asked my master.

'I knew they had one in their possession. It was cast in Dublin over fifty years ago and has seen action twice, proving itself to be a formidable weapon. The mages bought it and transported it here last year. But our spies report that they lack experienced gunners.'

The gun was dragged into position to the west of the castle. I studied the men clustered around it. At the siege of Malkin Tower, I remembered that the noise had been deafening, but I'd noted the skill of the gunners –

how they had worked as an efficient team, each performing his task with an economy of movement.

Amongst our armed defenders were about six or seven archers and, using their longbows, they now started to aim for the gunners. However, the distance was too great, the wind against them, and their arrows fell short.

I watched the heavy iron ball being rolled into the mouth of the cannon and the fuse being lit. By now the gunners were covering their ears.

There was a dull thud and a puff of smoke from the mouth of the cannon as the iron ball began its trajectory. It fell far short of the castle walls and skidded across the rough turf to end up in a clump of thistles. This brought a chorus of jeers from the defenders on the battlements.

It took the enemy about five minutes to fire the next shot. This one hit the wall of the castle very low down. There was a loud crack on impact, and a few fragments of stone fell onto the grass. It wasn't a good shot but this time there were no jeers. The next one again fell short, then after that every firing of the cannon resulted in a strike somewhere against the stone walls of the castle. The noise was unnerving, but no serious damage was being done to the stone.

Shey went off to talk to his men, patting each one on the back in turn. He was a good commander, attempting to keep up their morale.

'You have to be extremely accurate and hit the same point on the wall each time,' I pointed out to the Spook. 'These men lack the skill to make a breach.'

'Then let's hope they're not fast learners, lad,' he remarked, 'because they've plenty of round shot down there, and a week or so to improve their aim!'

It was true. In addition to barrels of water for cooling the cannon and many bags of gunpowder, there were dozens of pyramids of cannonballs stacked close to the big gun, and wagons of more ammunition waiting in the distance. All they lacked at present was the expertise to use their potentially dangerous weapon effectively.

After about an hour the gun fell silent, and a man

approached the castle gate. He was unarmed and carried a white flag which fluttered in the westerly wind. He stopped close to the gate and shouted his message up at us. He looked scared.

'My masters demand that you release the mage, Cormac, into our hands immediately. Do so and we will leave in peace. Failure to comply will result in dire consequences. We will batter down your walls, and everyone within will be put to the sword!'

Shey's face twitched with anger, and I watched the archers draw their bows and target the messenger, who was just seconds from death. But Shey gestured to them and they lowered their weapons.

'Go back and tell your masters that we refuse!' he shouted. 'Their time is almost over. This castle cannot be breached by the fools they have hired as gunners. Soon it will be your turn to be under siege. We will tear down your fort until not a stone remains standing.'

The messenger turned and walked back towards the ranks of our enemies. Within five minutes the gun began firing again.

* * *

The Spook decided that this was an opportunity for me to catch up on my studies. Late in the afternoon he was giving me a lesson – I was studying the history of the dark. The Spook had been telling me about a group of mages called the Kobalos, who supposedly lived far to the north. Though they stood upright, they were not human, and had the appearance of foxes or wolves. But there was little evidence that they really existed – only the jottings of one of the very first spooks – a man called Nicholas Browne. I had read about them already, and none of it was new to me, so I tried to get the Spook onto a subject that I found much more interesting. After all, we were dealing with hostile malevolent mages who worshipped Pan.

'What about Pan?' I asked. 'What do we know about him?'

The Spook pulled the Bestiary from his bag and leafed through until he came to the section on the Old Gods. He handed the book to me. 'Read that first and then ask your questions,' he commanded.

The entry on Pan was quite short and I read it quickly:

PAN (THE HORNED GOD)

Pan is the Old God, originally worshipped by the Greeks, who rules over nature and takes on two distinct physical forms. In one manifestation he is a boy and plays a set of reed pipes, his melodies so powerful that no birdsong can equal them and the very rocks move under their influence.

In his other form he is the terrifying deity of nature whose approach fills humans with terror – the word 'panic' is derived from his name. Now his sphere of influence has widened and he is worshipped by the goat mages of Ireland. After eight days of human sacrifice, Pan passes through a portal from the dark and briefly enters the body of a goat. He distorts the shape of that animal into a thing awful to behold . . .

'It's a really short entry,' I commented. 'We don't know very much about Pan, do we?'

'You're right there, lad,' my master replied, 'so we'll learn what we can while we're here. Things have changed since I wrote that. Now we know that the ceremony takes place twice a year rather than once. But what I've always found interesting is the duality of Pan. In one form he's a musician who seems almost benign. His other shape is terrifying and clearly belongs to the dark.'

'Why should there *be* such a thing as the dark?' I asked. 'How did it begin?'

'Nobody knows that for sure – we can only guess. I have little to add to the speculations I made in my Bestiary many years ago. But I still believe that the dark is fed by human wickedness. Human greed and lust for power make it ever stronger and more dangerous. If we could only change the hearts of men and women, the dark would be weakened – I'm sure of it. But I've lived long enough to know that it would be easier to hold back the tides than achieve that. We can only hope.'

'If we manage to bind the Fiend, it would be a start,' I suggested.

123

'It certainly would, lad.' The Spook frowned. 'Things couldn't be much worse than they are at present. Why, even Farrell Shey, an enemy of the dark, is prepared to use torture in order to prevail. It shows just how bad things have become.'

I suddenly realized that the cannon had fallen silent. 'The gun's stopped firing,' I said. 'Maybe it's overheated and the barrel's cracked.'

You needed lots of water to keep a barrel cool. If gunners became careless about that, a gun could even explode, killing all around it. Those men weren't experts. There was a real danger of that happening.

Before the Spook could reply, a messenger rapped on the door and came into the room without being invited. We were urgently summoned to the battlements.

As we climbed the stairs, we were jostled by armed men, who were also on their way up. Something must be afoot – was it some new threat?

Alice was already up there; she came towards us as we blinked into the sun, which was sinking towards the sea. She shielded her eyes and pointed. 'The mages are gathered around the gun,' she said. 'They're up to something. Shey is really worried.'

No sooner had she mentioned his name than the landowner strode across to us, the soldiers on the battlements stepping aside to allow him through. 'I think they're going to attempt some type of magic,' he told us. 'There was little danger of them harnessing the dark in Killorglin because we only faced two of them. There are nine now, and they are combining their strength . . .'

I looked down towards the cannon. The mages had formed a circle around it. Then I realized that the focus of their attention wasn't the big gun itself: the gunners were kneeling, and the mages were laying their hands on their heads and shoulders. They were transferring power to them in some way. What kind of power? I wondered. The knowledge and skills of expert gunners? It seemed likely.

On the battlements the defenders had fallen silent. But we could hear the wind from the sea sighing in the distance, and the faint chanting of the mages. Waves of cold ran up and down my spine. Even at that distance I was able to detect the use of dark magic. It was strong and dangerous.

Just *how* dangerous we found out ten minutes later, when the cannon started up again. The gunners' first shot made a direct hit on the wall, low and just to the left of the main gate. So did the second and the third. They were striking almost exactly the same spot with each cannonball. Even in the hour before dark we could see clear damage. The wall was thick, but the outer layer of stones was already beginning to break away. There was a small mound of debris on the grass below.

Darkness brought respite from the assault, but it would no doubt resume at dawn, and it seemed to me that they might well breach the wall by the next sunset.

CHAPTER 8
THIN SHAUN

Dawn brought cloud and the approach of rain, but the mages' gunners recommenced their attack with their new-found accuracy. Though now the wind was blowing from the south rather than directly from behind the gun, our archers were able to rain arrows down in the vicinity of the weapon, causing a delay of about an hour while it was repositioned out of range.

That greater distance made no difference to the aim of the gunners, however, and the same point on the wall was subjected to a heavy pounding, cannonballs striking the same spot about every five minutes, with longer pauses while they used water to cool the weapon.

By late afternoon the situation had become critical: a small hole had been punched right through the castle wall. According to Shey, it would not take much further damage to undermine the battlements above, creating a heap of stones beside the gate over which our attackers could swarm to capture the castle.

In desperation, he led a force of about twenty mounted men through the main gate; they charged directly towards the gun, intending to kill the gunners. They were intercepted first by enemy riders and then by foot soldiers. Despite the enemy's defences, things seemed to be going their way: Shey's men were gaining ground, fighting their way towards the gun. Within a couple of minutes they would have achieved their aim, but then someone intervened.

A large muscular man with a shaven head and goatee beard joined the fray. He carried a huge double-bladed battle-axe and used it with deadly effect. He cut two of our soldiers down from their horses, each with a single blow, and immediately the tide turned. Our enemies fought with renewed vigour, and Shey was forced to improvise a retreat back towards the gate. It was barely closed before the enemy were at the walls.

They didn't stay long. The Alliance archers killed and wounded a few; the rest withdrew behind their gunners. I'd expected them to commence firing again right away, but instead the large man approached the gate alone. He carried no white flag but had that huge axe resting on his shoulder. Unlike the messenger, he looked confident and walked with a swagger.

Shey climbed back up to the battlements and stood beside the Spook. 'That's Magister Doolan, the Butcher, the leader of the mages,' he told him.

Doolan halted right below and glared up at us. 'Who will come down and fight me?' he taunted, his powerful voice booming upwards.

He received no reply and gave a long derisory laugh. 'You're cowards, all of you. There's not one real man amongst you!' he cried, and began to strut up and down before the walls, waving his axe at us in challenge.

'Kill him!' Shey commanded his archers.

They began to loose arrows at him. He was without armour and looked certain to die. But for some reason the arrows all missed or fell short. Was he using some sort of magic against them? If the mages could, with a spell, make novice gunners into experts, no doubt they could do the opposite. Then one arrow sped directly towards its target and seemed certain to bury itself in the big man's heart, but he twirled his large battle-axe as if it were lighter than a feather and deflected the arrow harmlessly to the ground.

With another laugh, he turned his back and casually returned to his own lines; each arrow loosed after him fell well short. Immediately the enemy gunners began to fire again.

Eventually the light began to fail and the gunners stopped pounding the weak point on the western wall, but we knew that the next day would be critical: a full attack on the castle was expected as soon as that wall collapsed.

Soon after dark we had a meeting with Shey.

'The castle will fall tomorrow – probably shortly after dawn,' he admitted. 'I suggest that as soon as the wall is breached, you make your escape, taking our prisoner with you. I can spare four soldiers to accompany you. I'll stay here with the remainder of my men. We'll make a fight of it and sell our lives dearly.'

The Spook nodded gravely. 'Aye, that seems the best option,' he said. 'But won't we be seen?'

'There's a small secret gate to the south, hidden by bushes and a mound of earth. The enemy's attention will be on the breach. You've a good chance of getting away.'

'We need to keep the mage alive and out of their hands,' said the Spook. 'Where should we make for? Is there another refuge?'

'No – you need to get back to my home in Kenmare – that's the safest place.' Shey shook his head and sighed. 'But it won't be easy. You face a hazardous journey. To the south and east there are extensive boglands. I suggest you make for the river Inny. Then follow it upstream into the mountains. My men know the way. They'll guide you through, passing well north of Staigue and avoiding the fort. Then back southeast to Kenmare again.'

'Wouldn't it be better to do it now, long before dawn?' I suggested. 'You say that the gate is well hidden, but the mages' spies may know of it. We'd have a far better chance under cover of darkness.'

Alice smiled in approval, but for a moment I thought the Spook was about to dismiss my idea; then he scratched his beard and nodded. 'The lad could well be right,' he said, turning to Shey. 'Would that present a problem?'

'Not at all. We could have you away within the hour.'

So we made our preparations. The mage was brought up from his cell and secured with rope, his arms bound to his sides. He was also blindfolded and gagged so that he was unable to call for help, but his legs were left free. That done, we took our leave of Shey and wished him good fortune in the coming battle.

We were led to the southern gate by the four soldiers assigned as our escort; after climbing the stone steps up to it, they listened carefully for any sounds of activity outside. Satisfied that all was clear, they signalled to the leader of a small squad of armed troops who were standing by. This force was stationed here to prevent an attack on the gate from the outside.

Their leader unlocked the metal door with a large key. It opened inwards, and he eased it back to reveal a covering of soil and rocks. Two of his men stepped forward with spades and quickly cut their way through it; cool air suddenly wafted into our faces.

As they worked, the Spook looked at each of us in turn and spoke, his voice hardly more than a whisper. 'If things go wrong and we get separated, meet up at the river.'

It was pitch-dark now. As we could use neither torches nor lanterns, it was vital to stick close together. There was a mound of earth about five paces from the gate – to hide it from distant observers – but there was still a chance that enemy soldiers were waiting just beyond it. What if the mages had discovered the existence of the secret gate? A powerful

Pendle witch might certainly have sniffed it out.

This was a moment of danger, and the four soldiers went out first, climbing the steep slope to seek cover in the screen of bushes at the top. We listened, but all was silent. Our avenue of escape was clear. The Spook pushed the stumbling prisoner ahead of him, and Alice and I followed. We knelt down on the grass, listening to the sound of the door being locked behind us.

We were on our own now; if attacked, we could expect no help from those within the castle. We climbed the slope and crouched alongside our escort. There were fires visible in the distance to the south, west and east. The enemy completely encircled us, but there were gaps between those campfires, some larger than others. A few of the enemy would be on guard duty, alert for danger, but hopefully most would be asleep.

We began to crawl down the hill, one after the other. At the bottom we crept forward, three of our escort to the fore, the Spook next with the fourth soldier, carrying the prisoner between them. Alice was just behind them, with me bringing up the rear.

Every few minutes we came to a halt and lay perfectly still, face down on the damp ground. After about fifteen minutes of this we were almost level with the ring of fires that encircled the castle. We were midway between two, each about fifty paces away. I could see a sentry standing in front of a shelter made from animal skins stretched over a wooden frame. There were also men in the open – those who couldn't be accommodated in the tent – sleeping close to the warmth of the fire.

This was the part of our escape that carried the greatest risk. If we were seen now, dozens of armed men would reach us in seconds. Once again we set off, leaving the fires behind now, the welcome darkness waiting to swallow us and hide us from our enemies.

Again we rested and lay face down in the dark. But then, as we began to crawl forward again, one of our soldiers stifled a cough. Instantly we froze. I glanced back to my left, and saw that the sentry outside the nearest tent was coming towards us. I held my breath. He halted but continued to stare in our direction. I could hear the soldier ahead of me spluttering and choking. He was fighting the almost irresistible urge to cough. Failure to do so would put all our lives in jeopardy.

He lost the battle, and let out a loud explosive sound. The sentry shouted something and, drawing his sword, began to run towards us. There were other shouts, and more enemy soldiers joined him. We got to our feet and began to sprint away. Our only hope was to lose our pursuers in the darkness.

Our escort had fled for their lives, so we ran too. For a few moments Alice was running just ahead of me, but then I passed the Spook, who was struggling with Cormac, the captive mage. I grabbed the man's other shoulder, and together my master and I dragged him forward. But it was hopeless. When I glanced back, I could see flickering torches and hear the pounding of feet. They were catching us fast. The going underfoot was getting worse. The ground was uneven and I kept splashing through water. We were entering the bog.

No doubt there were safe paths through it, but we

were scattered now, our guides somewhere ahead, and I feared we could blunder into dangerous ground that might suck us in. The greatest threat was now close on our heels and, acting simultaneously and instinctively, the Spook and I released the prisoner, pushing him to his knees, and spun, staffs at the ready, to face our attackers.

I remember wondering where Alice was: she was unarmed and couldn't stand and fight, but neither could she afford to wander too far from the protection of the blood jar. Then I had to focus on the immediate threat. A bearded mage brandishing a sword in his right hand and a torch in his left ran straight at me, aiming a blow at my head, his mouth stretched wide to show his teeth; he looked like a wild animal.

Ignoring the sword, I jabbed the base of my staff towards his forehead. The blow struck home, its force aided by his forward momentum. He went down, the sword spinning out of his hand. But there were more armed men, and then they were all around us. For a few moments I stood back to back with my master.

Again almost simultaneously we pressed the buttons on our staffs and used our retractable blades. Now it was kill or be killed. We fought desperately, whirling and jabbing, but then, under pressure from the attack, we became separated.

Threatened from every side and with nobody to guard my back, I was already starting to tire; the attack was relentless. I thought it was all over for me, but then I saw my chance. Three soldiers were pressing me hard, but only one carried a torch. I knocked it out of his hand and it fell, extinguishing itself on impact with the waterlogged ground, plunging us into darkness.

In the confusion, I made for what I thought was southeast towards the river Inny. The Spook had told us to meet up there if things went wrong. Well, they'd gone wrong all right, and I was increasingly worried about Alice. If she was too far from the blood jar, the Fiend would come for her.

Our attempt to escape with our hostage had been a disaster. We were scattered and on the run, and the mages had surely rescued him. Now they would go ahead with the ceremony. Dark times lay ahead for the Alliance.

At one point I paused and glanced back, listening intently. There were no signs of pursuit, but my eyes had adjusted to the dark now and I could see the distant campfires, no more than tiny pinpoints of light in the darkness. So I continued more cautiously, using my staff to test the depth of the water ahead. On more than one occasion it saved me from drowning or being sucked down into the bog. Even so, I was constantly tripping over big tussocks of marsh grass or plunging up to my knees in ice-cold stinking water.

My memory of Shey's map gave me few clues as to how long the journey should take, and the going was difficult. I remembered that I needed to keep well north of the mountains in order to reach the river. Apart from that my knowledge of the terrain was vague, but I knew that somewhere on the southern edge of the hills was the Staigue ring fort. Some of the mages and their servants would still be there – it was a place to be avoided at all costs.

* * *

It was hard to judge the passage of time, but eventually the sky ahead started to grow lighter and I knew it wouldn't be long before dawn. I'd hoped that would enable me to take my bearings from the mountains and find the river, but it wasn't to be. Soon tendrils of mist were snaking towards me, and I quickly became enveloped in a dense fog. The air was still, and apart from the sound of my own breathing and my boots squelching through the bog, all was silent.

Later, in the early dawn light, I saw a cottage looming up before me through the mist. A tall thin man carrying a spade over his shoulder came out of the door. He was wearing a jacket with a hood, not unlike my own, but no hair was visible on his forehead. From a distance, he looked like a turf-cutter setting off for a hard day's work, eager to make the best of the winter's short daylight hours. He came across to intercept me and gave me a broad smile. It was then that I noticed how pale his narrow face was. It was not the face of someone who worked outdoors.

'You look lost, boy. Where are you heading?' he demanded, his voice as harsh as the croak of an old bullfrog. The skin was stretched tight across his cheek-bones; from close up, it looked a little yellow, as though he'd recently been ill. His eyes were deep-set, as if they were sinking into his skull, droopy eyelids and folds of skin closing over them.

'I'm making for the river,' I told him. 'I'm supposed to meet some friends there.'

'You're slightly off track – you should be heading that way,' he said, pointing in what seemed to be a more easterly direction. 'Have you been walking all night?'

I nodded.

'Well, in that case you'll be cold and hungry. Mistress Scarabek will make you something to eat and let you warm yourself by the fire for a while,' he said, indicating the front door of the cottage. 'Knock quietly so as not to wake the young 'un, and ask her for some break-fast. Tell her that Thin Shaun sent you.'

The man's appearance was odd, but I was in urgent

need of food and shelter. I nodded my thanks, approached the cottage and rapped lightly on the door, trying to make as little noise as possible.

I heard the slip-slap of bare feet and the door opened a crack. It was dark inside, but I thought I could make out a single unblinking eye.

'Thin Shaun sent me,' I said, keeping my voice low so as not to wake the child. 'He said you'd give me a little breakfast, please. If that's not too much - trouble . . .'

For what seemed like an age there was no response, but then the door opened silently and I saw a woman wearing a green woollen shawl. This must be Mistress Scarabek, I thought. She looked sad and, like Shaun, had very pale skin, with red-rimmed eyes that suggested she'd either been crying recently or had been up all night. The baby had probably kept her awake.

'Come in,' she said, her voice gentle. I remember thinking what a contrast it was to Thin Shaun's croaky rasp. 'But leave your staff outside. We'll have no need for spook's work in here.'

Thinking nothing of it, I obeyed without question, leaning my staff against the wall next to the window and stepping into the cottage. It was small and cosy, with a turf fire glowing in the grate. Two stools faced the hearth, and against the wall stood a small cradle on rockers; before going through to the kitchen, Scarabek set the thing in motion to keep the baby happy.

A few moments later she returned carrying a small bowl, which she handed to me. 'Here – that's all I have, a little gruel. We're poor people. Times are hard and I must think of my family's needs.'

I thanked her and started to eat the thin porridge with my fingers. It was cold and a little slimy, but after what she'd just said I tried not to betray my dislike of it. It didn't really taste unpleasant – just a little odd, with a spicy tang. But strangely it made my mouth very dry.

'Thank you,' I said when I'd finished the gruel, taking care to eat up every last bit. 'I don't suppose I could trouble you for a cup of water?'

'You don't need water,' Scarabek said mysteriously.

'Why don't you lie down in front of the fire and rest your young bones until it gets dark?'

The stone flags were hard and cold, despite the proximity of the fire, but I suddenly felt very tired and what she suggested seemed a good idea. So I stretched before the hearth.

'Close your eyes,' Scarabek commanded. 'That would be wise. It'll be better for us all once it's gone dark.'

I remember thinking her words were really odd and I felt confused. What did she mean? How could the dark be 'better for us all'? Moreover, the sun couldn't have been up for more than half an hour or so. It would be another nine hours before it got dark. Did she expect me to lie here all that time? And wasn't there something I had to do? I had to meet somebody. But I couldn't remember who or where.

CHAPTER 9
SMALL COLD FINGERS

I opened my eyes; it was dark in the cottage and I felt stiff and cold. The fire was out but there was a candle burning on the mantelpiece.

I felt utterly weary and wanted to close my eyes and drift back into a deep sleep. I was about to do just that when I saw something that made me gasp with concern. The baby's cradle had fallen over and was lying on its side!

There was the infant, half in, half out of it, still wrapped in a woollen blanket. I tried to call out for its mother, but when I opened my mouth, all that came out was a faint croak. I realized then that I was breathing rapidly; my heart was fluttering in my chest with a scary irregular beat that made me fear it was about to stop at any minute. I was unable to move my limbs.

Was I seriously ill? I wondered. Had I caught some type of fever in the bog-lands?

Then I thought I saw the baby's blanket move. It gave a sort of twitch, then began to rise and fall rhythmically, suggesting that the child was still breathing and had survived the fall. I tried to call for the mother again, but could still only manage a weak cry; the effort sent my heart into such a speedy fluttering rhythm that I began to tremble all over, fearing that I was dying.

I suddenly realized that the woollen blanket was now moving in a different way. It seemed to be coming slowly towards me. How old was the baby? Was it old enough to crawl like that? Even though it was completely covered by the blanket and couldn't possibly see where it was going, it was heading directly for me. Could it hear my breathing? Was it seeking comfort? Why didn't Scarabek come to check on it?

Then I heard a strange sound. It was coming from the

baby. Despite the utter silence of the room I could hear no breathing – only a sort of rhythmical clicking. It sounded like gnashing teeth. Suddenly I was scared. Babies that small didn't have teeth!

No, it had to be something else. The moment that thought entered my head, a cold tremor ran the length of my spine, a warning that something from the dark was very close. I desperately tried to move my limbs, but they were still paralysed. I lay there, watching it helplessly.

As the baby approached me, the woollen blanket seemed to convulse, and I heard a big gasp, as if whatever it was beneath the blanket had been holding its breath for a very long time and now desperately needed energy for some immense effort.

It reached my foot, and came to a halt for a few moments. Once again I heard what sounded like another huge in-breath, but this time I identified the sound; my first guess had been wrong. It was sniffing – sniffing like a witch, gathering information about me. It left my boot and began to move up along my body, pausing beside my chest. Once again it sniffed very loudly.

I shuddered as it then climbed slowly up onto my chest. I was aware of four small limbs moving across me. Even through my clothes they felt very cold, like four blocks of ice. Whatever it was had finally reached my face now and I began to panic: my heart pounded even more wildly. What was it? What horrible thing was hidden beneath that moving blanket?

I tried to roll away onto my side, but couldn't find the strength. All I could do was to raise my head a little. Nor could I manage to fend it off with my hands – they trembled uselessly at my sides while rivulets of sweat ran down my forehead into my eyes. I was unable to defend myself.

It had reached my throat now, and raised itself up a little on its tiny hands as if to peer into my face, causing the blanket to fall back so that, simultaneously, I saw its face too.

I expected to see a monster and my fears were fully realized – but not in the way I expected.

The head was no larger than that of a baby of two or three months, but it had the face of a little old man; it was malevolent, filled with some desperate need. And it looked very like Thin Shaun, the turf-cutter who had sent me here for food. And I suddenly understood that although I'd been fed, given a little gruel, *I* was also food – nourishment for this grotesque being. What I'd eaten must have contained some sleeping draught to render me weak and helpless. Now the creature's mouth opened wide, revealing long needle-like teeth, and they were aiming for my throat.

I felt its small cold fingers on my neck; then a sudden sharp stab of pain as the teeth punctured my flesh. It began to suck noisily, and I felt the blood being drawn out of my body – and with it my life.

I had no strength to resist. There was little pain, just a sense of floating away towards death. How long it went on I have no idea, but the next thing I knew, Scarabek was walking purposefully into the room, her shadow flickering on the ceiling in the candlelight. She came across and gently plucked the creature from me;

as it came away, I felt a tugging at my throat when its teeth were withdrawn. She carried it over to the cradle, which still lay on its side, and swaddled it in the woollen blanket again.

She started singing to it in a low voice – a lullaby that might have been used to soothe a human child. Then she righted the cradle and placed the creature inside, carefully adjusting the blanket to keep it warm.

Scarabek came back and stared down at me, and I saw that her face had changed. Previously, she must have used some enchantment to disguise herself. The truth was now revealed and I recognized her instantly. There was no doubt: she was the Celtic witch from my dreams. These were the eyes – one green, the other blue – that I had seen in the cloud as we'd approached Ireland and when we faced the jibber in Dublin, and I shuddered at the malevolence glaring from them.

But how was it possible? How could she have returned from the dead when the dogs had eaten her heart?

'Tom Ward! How easily you fell into my hands! Ever

since you approached our shore I have been watching and waiting!' she cried. 'It took the *simplest* of spells to lure you into my cottage. And how well you obeyed me, leaving your precious staff at the threshold. Now you are totally in my power. My life will end soon, my spirit given up in sacrifice to Pan. You will die too, but only after suffering terribly for what you did to my sister.'

Sisters . . . Were they twins? They looked so alike. I wanted to ask her, but I was almost too weak to draw breath. How much blood had the little creature taken? I wondered. I fought to remain conscious, but my head began to spin and I fell into darkness. The witch had promised to make me suffer, but I already felt close to death – although there was no fear; just a terrible weariness.

How long I was unconscious I don't know, but when I came to, I heard voices: a man and a woman talking together quietly. I tried to make sense of what they were saying – something about barrows and travelling north. At last I managed to find the strength to open my eyes. The two of them were standing over me – Scarabek, the witch, and the man called Thin Shaun.

But was he really a man or something else? His hood was pulled back, revealing an emaciated head that could almost have been that of a corpse. The skull was clearly visible, the skin thin and parchment dry, his hairless head covered in patches of dry, flaking skin.

'He conceals a deadly weapon in the left pocket of his cloak,' said Scarabek. 'Take it from him, Shaun. I cannot bear to touch it.'

Thin Shaun reached into my pocket. I had no strength to resist, and he drew out my silver chain. As he did so, I saw the pain upon his face: with a shudder, he dropped it on the ground, out of my reach.

'He used that to bind my sister before she was slain. But he won't ever need to use it again. His life as an apprentice spook is over. We'll take him north now, Shaun,' said the witch. 'I'm going to hurt him badly and let him feel something of the suffering I experienced.'

I was dismayed at the loss of my silver chain, but at least he hadn't discovered the blood jar in my pocket.

Thin Shaun came across, picked me up and threw me over his shoulder, just as my master would carry a bound witch before putting her into a pit. He held me by the legs so that my head was hanging down towards his heels. I lacked the strength to resist, and was aware of a strange musty smell emanating from him, an odour of dank underground places. But what really unnerved me was the extreme coldness of his body; even though I could feel and hear him breathing, it was as if I was being carried by a dead man.

Curiously, though my body was weak, my mind became strangely alert. I tried to practise what the Spook had taught me and take careful note of my situation.

We left the cottage and headed north, Scarabek taking the lead and carrying the creature in the woollen shawl close to her bosom as if it were a human baby. Perhaps it was her familiar. A witch usually gave a familiar her own blood, but this was often augmented by blood from her victims. The most common familiars were cats, rats, birds and toads, but sometimes witches used something more exotic. I had no name for the thing she was carrying; it certainly wasn't mentioned in the Spook's Bestiary. But I was dealing with a witch from a foreign land, and her powers and habits were largely unknown to me.

To the east the sky was already becoming lighter. I must have slept for at least a day and a night. The fog was lifting and I could see the bulk of two mountains rising up ahead and to the right. And then I caught sight of something else – the unmistakable shape of a burial mound – and we were moving directly towards it. It was small, hardly more than twice the height of a man, and covered in grass. When we were less than five yards away, there was an intense flash of yellow light. As it dimmed, I saw the silhouette of the witch against a round doorway.

Moments later, the breeze died down and the air immediately became significantly warmer; we were surrounded by darkness, right inside the barrow. There was sudden flare of light and I saw that the witch was holding a black candle, which she'd just ignited by magic. Within the mound stood a table, four chairs and a bed, to which she pointed.

'Put him there for now,' she instructed, and Thin Shaun dumped me on it without ceremony. 'It's time to feed him again . . .'

I lay there for several minutes, struggling to move. I was still suffering from that strange paralysis. The witch had gone into another room within the barrow, but Shaun stood there silently, his unblinking eyes staring down at me. I was starting to feel a little stronger, and my heart and breathing were gradually returning to normal. But I guessed that Scarabek was now going to feed me more of the gruel laced with poison. If only I could manage to regain the full use of my limbs.

She returned within minutes, carrying a small bowl. 'Lift his head, Shaun,' she commanded.

With his right hand, Thin Shaun gripped my shoulder, lifting the top part of my body almost upright. This time the witch had a small wooden spoon, and as she brought it towards me, she held my forehead firmly while, with his left hand, Shaun tugged my jaw downwards, forcing my mouth wide open.

The witch kept stuffing the spicy gruel into my mouth until I was forced to either swallow or choke. As the concoction went down my gullet, she smiled.

'That's enough for now – let him go,' she said. 'Too much will kill him, and I have other plans for him first.'

Thin Shaun lowered me back onto the bed and stood beside Scarabek. They stared down at me while my mouth grew dry and the room started to spin.

'Let's go out and get the girl,' I heard the witch say. 'He'll be safe enough here.'

The girl – *Which girl?* I wondered. Did they mean Alice? But then, once again, I felt my heart flutter and I fell into darkness. I knew no more for a while but kept having dreams of flying and falling. For some strange reason I was compelled to jump from a cliff, spreading my arms wide like a bird's wings. But then I would plunge downwards out of a dark sky, the unseen ground rushing up to meet me.

I felt someone shaking me roughly by the shoulder; then cold water was dashed into my face. I opened my eyes to see Thin Shaun staring down and smell his foul breath. He stepped back to reveal that there were two other people in the room. One was the witch; the other was Alice.

My heart lurched. Alice looked dishevelled and her hands were bound behind her back.

'Oh, Tom!' she cried. 'What have they done to you? You look so ill—'

But the witch interrupted. 'Worry about yourself, child!' she cried. 'Your time on this earth is almost over. Within the hour I will give you to your father, the Fiend.'

CHAPTER
10

IN THE GRASP OF THE FIEND

As Thin Shaun picked me up again, I heard Scarabek cry some word of dark magic. Seconds later we were standing outside the burial mound. It was dark once more, and there was a waxing crescent moon; the air was very cold, a hoar frost already forming over the soft boggy ground.

We headed north, the witch's fist bunched in Alice's hair as she dragged her along. The familiar had been left behind in the barrow.

Alice had been beyond the protection of the blood jar, so why, I wondered, hadn't the Fiend come for her already? We'd both expected that, at the first opportunity, he'd take his revenge.

So was the witch going to summon him now? If so, the blood jar would prevent him from coming near. Did she know about it? Would she break it and give us both to the Fiend?

The landscape was bleak and treeless but covered with scrub and brambles, and it was to a tangled thicket that the witch finally led us. She dragged Alice over to a large thorny bush and tied her by the hair to its intertwined branches. While I watched from Thin Shaun's shoulder, horrified at what was taking place, Scarabek circled the bramble patch three times against the clock, chanting dark spells. Alice began to weep. Her knowledge of the craft would tell her exactly what the witch was doing.

'Oh, Tom!' Alice cried. 'She's done a deal with the Fiend. She wants to hurt you too. He'll be here soon.'

'He will indeed!' agreed Scarabek. 'So it's time to get you yonder so that the Fiend can come and collect the girl. Let's away!' she commanded Thin Shaun.

I'd expected – and hoped – to be tied up alongside

Alice. Unknown to the witch, I still had the blood jar in my pocket, so he surely couldn't hurt me.

But I was led away from Alice, up the slope. We gazed back down from on high. Alice looked very tiny, but I could just make out her desperate struggles to get free of the brambles.

I soon found out how wrong I'd been about Scarabek: she knew everything!

'We're far enough away now,' she said, 'and the girl's beyond the protection of that jar she made. So that's the first pain you'll endure – watching the Fiend take your pretty friend's life and soul! He's delighted to have the opportunity to make you suffer. But don't worry, I won't let him get his hands on *you*! I intend to give you to the Morrigan.'

Lightning suddenly split the sky to the west as dark clouds raced inland, obscuring the stars. It was followed within seconds by a rumble of thunder, and then, in the ensuing silence, I heard a new sound – that of distant but very heavy footfalls, each followed by an explosive hiss.

Although still mostly invisible, the Fiend was just starting to materialize. He would take on the huge form of what witches called 'his fearsome majesty', a shape designed to instil fear and awe in all who beheld him. Some said that the sight could make you die of fear on the spot. No doubt this was true for those of a nervous disposition, but I had been close to him in that form before, and so had Alice, and we'd both survived the encounter.

We were too far away to see his approaching footprints. They were fiery hot, and whereas his cloven hooves could burn their impression into wooden floorboards, in cold boggy terrain like this they would merely cause the ground to spit and hiss, erupting in spurts of steam at each contact.

Although the clouds were almost halfway across the sky now, the moon was still ahead of that dark advancing curtain, and by its light I saw the Fiend materialize fully. Even at this distance he looked huge: thick and muscular, his torso shaped like a barrel, his whole body covered in hair as thick as the hide of an ox. Huge horns curved from his head and his tail snaked upwards in an arc behind him.

My heart was in my mouth as he strode directly towards Alice, who was struggling in vain to tear herself free of the brambles. I could hear her screams of terror. I tried to struggle out of Thin Shaun's grip, but he was very strong and, in my weakened condition, my efforts were feeble.

Towering above Alice, the Fiend reached down with his huge left hand and knotted his fist in her hair, as the witch had done, tearing her free of the brambles and lifting her up so that her face was level with his own. She screamed again as her hair was ripped from the thicket, and began to weep. The Fiend loomed closer, as if intending to bite off her head.

'Tom! Tom!' she cried. 'Goodbye, Tom. Goodbye!'

At those words my heart surged up into my mouth and I could hardly breathe. Was this it? Was it really over at last? The Fiend had her in his clutches, and there was nothing more I could do to save her. But how would I live without Alice? Tears began to run down my face and I began to sob uncontrollably. It was the pain of imminent loss, yes, but also the pangs that came from my empathy with Alice.

We were so close I knew exactly what she was experiencing. I suffered what she suffered. Never again to be comfortable in this world; anticipating an eternity of pain and terror as her soul languished in the dark, at the mercy of the Fiend, who would devise endless tortures to repay her for the trouble and hurt she had caused him because of me. All because of me. It was just too much to bear.

A moment later it was over. There was a flash of light, a rumble of thunder, and a blast of hot wind searing into our faces. I screwed up my eyes, and when I was able to open them again, the Fiend had vanished, taking Alice with him.

Another pang of loss knotted my stomach. Alice was now beyond this world; never had I felt so alone. As Thin Shaun carried me, Scarabek walked close beside me, spitting cruel taunts.

Although she grinned with delight at my tears,

which flowed as copiously as the rain that swept over us, I cared nothing for her heartless words. My tears were for Alice and for myself. Now the world had changed terribly. I had lost my mam and dad, and both losses had been devastating, but this was different. This was a pain beyond even that. I had called Alice my friend, held hands with her, sat beside her. But only now that she was snatched away for ever did I fully realize the truth.

I loved Alice, and now she was gone.

After collecting the creature from the barrow, we returned to the cottage, and Thin Shaun threw me onto the bed like a sack of rotten potatoes.

Scarabek looked at me with scorn. 'Even if you weep an ocean,' she hissed, 'your sorrow will not even be able to approach mine. I loved my sister as myself, for indeed she was me and I her!'

'What do you mean?' I demanded. Despite my anguish, the spook in me was waiting just below the surface. My master had taught me to use every opportunity to learn about our enemies so as to be in a better position to eventually defeat them.

'We were twins,' she answered. 'Witch-twins of a type so rare that only once before has our like been seen in this land. We shared one mind – a mind controlling two bodies. I looked out through her eyes and she through mine.'

'But your eyes are not the same as hers. One is blue and the other is green – why should that be so?' I asked curiously.

'Once both my eyes were blue, but since my sister's death I have wandered among the Hollow Hills, seeking power,' the witch replied. 'All who stay too long there are changed. But we were closer than you can ever imagine. The experiences she had, I had too. The pain she felt, I felt too. I was there when you betrayed and killed her. Half of me was ripped away at her death.'

'If you were there, then you will know I didn't kill her,' I protested. 'It was my master, Bill Arkwright.'

'Don't lie! You were working together. You planned her death. It was a trick – your device.'

I shook my head weakly. 'That's not true. I would have kept my side of the bargain.'

'Why should I believe a spook's apprentice? What you say matters little and will make no difference to what I plan.'

'What are you going to do with me now?' I asked. It was better to know the worst. Despite my grief, I was still calculating the odds against me – searching for any chance of escape, however slim. My silver chain was still on the floor where Thin Shaun had cast it. But when I looked at it out of the corner of my eye, Scarabek gave me an evil smile.

'Forget that. Your days of wielding such a weapon are over. You will be too weak to use it, being food for Konal. He'll be hungry again within the hour.'

'Konal is your familiar?'

The witch shook her head. 'No, Konal is my beloved son, and his father is Thin Shaun, the barrow keeper, whose time on this earth is now short. A keeper has only one son, born of a witch – the child who will replace him and continue his role.'

'The keeper? Why is he called that?'

'The name is apt. Keepers maintain the many barrows that are scattered across our land. Once they contained the bones of the ancient dead, but now they are refuges for the Celtic witches. Shaun keeps the magic strong and appeases those who made them, for their spirits are never far away. He offers them blood.'

A horrible thought struck me. Did Thin Shaun need blood like his son? I glanced up at the keeper, who gave me an evil smile.

'I can see the fear in your face,' he told me. 'You think I seek to drain you too? Am I right?'

I shrank away from him. Could he read my mind?

'Well, you needn't fear on that account,' Thin Shaun said. 'I offer up the blood of animals. Only rarely does a keeper take human blood. But then, if his thirst is great, he drains his victims until they are dead.'

'But none of this concerns you, who have perhaps less than a week to live,' the witch interrupted. 'Soon we'll be in Killorglin and your suffering will intensify. We've talked enough. Shaun, bring more gruel!'

They force-fed me again, this time a smaller amount; then, while I lay there, helpless, my mouth dry, a gritty feeling in my throat, the world beginning to spin, the witch brought her child over to where I lay. She partially unwrapped it from the blanket and laid Konal close to my neck. Within moments I felt the stab of its sharp teeth, and while Scarabek watched over me, smiling, my blood was slowly drained.

My thoughts were still all of Alice's fate, and the grief was in my throat and chest, almost choking me. It was a relief to grow weaker, the poisoned gruel and slow loss of blood plunging me into a merciful unconsciousness.

CHAPTER 11

THE KILLORGLIN GOAT

I remember very little. We must have used horses – as if from a great distance, I heard the sound of hooves, and my body was repeatedly jolted and shaken. Whether I was in a cart or tied over the back of a pony I'm not sure – maybe, over the duration of the journey, both.

My next clear recollection was of sitting on a heap of dirty straw in a dusty attic. It was full of rubbish, and curtained with enormous cobwebs strewn with desiccated fly carcasses; spiders were coiled in dark corners, ready to spring upon their next victim. There was daylight coming through the only window – a sky-light set in the sloping ceiling directly above me. I could hear the squawking and pattering of seagulls walking on the roof. I was alone in the room, my hands tied behind my back – though my legs were free.

I felt shaky, but at the second attempt managed to struggle to my feet. I could hear other noises: the occasional *clip-clop* of hooves, and people shouting in the sing-song manner of market traders. I suspected that I was now back in Killorglin. I leaned against the door handle, but it was locked, so I moved around the attic, looking for something I could use to help me escape. Perhaps there was something sharp to cut through my bonds . . .

I'd no sooner started my search than the room went dark. Was there a heavy cloud overhead blotting out the sun? Was a storm approaching? I wondered. The street sounds had also gradually faded away until I could hear nothing beyond the walls of my prison: I was trapped in a cocoon of silence.

Next the temperature began to drop; it warned me that something from the dark was approaching. I sat down in a corner with my back against the wall so that nothing could come at me from behind. I'd no weapons I could use to defend myself. If only my hands were free, I thought. Having them bound made me feel vulnerable.

Something started to whisper in my ear. At first I thought it might be a jibber, and my whole body started to shake with fear, but then I realized it was some other type of spirit. Its words were half formed and unintelligible but they had a malevolent force. Moments later it was joined by others – how many, I couldn't be sure, but the entities were close and I saw flashes of baleful purple light as they circled the gloomy attic, approaching nearer and nearer. Thin fingers began to tug at my ears, and then powerful hands clamped themselves about my throat and began to squeeze. It was a strangler ghost, a powerful one, and I was helpless against it.

A seventh son of a seventh son has some immunity against such dangerous spirits, but I'd never encountered one as strong; I began to choke as my windpipe was constricted by invisible fingers. I struggled to breathe, trying to think of something from my training that might help me. I gasped, feeling my consciousness ebbing away.

But then, all of a sudden, the pressure on my throat eased and the whispering voices fell mercifully silent. However, my respite lasted just seconds because one deep terrifying voice replaced them – that of the Fiend.

'I have your little friend Alice here with me now,' he taunted me. 'Would you like to hear her?'

Before I could answer I heard someone sobbing. The sounds seemed to reach me from a great distance, but I was listening to a girl crying. Was it indeed Alice or was it some trick of the Fiend? It was not for nothing that one of his titles was the Father of Lies.

'She is scared and she is suffering, Tom. Do you doubt it? Soon you will join her. I can almost reach you now. You are close – so very, very close.'

That was true enough. I couldn't actually see him, but I could feel his hot, fetid breath in my face and sense the proximity of something huge and terrifying.

The Fiend was crouching over me, straining to grab hold of me.

'Would you like to talk to your friend, Tom? Perhaps hearing your voice will ease her suffering a little . . .' he rasped.

Against my better judgement I called out to her. I just couldn't bear to hear her crying in the dark like that.

'Alice! Alice! It's me, Tom,' I shouted. 'Hold on, be strong. Somehow I'll get you out of there! I'll bring you home!'

'Liar!' Alice shouted. 'Don't lie to me. You're not Tom. I've been deceived enough!'

'It is me, Alice, I swear it.'

'Devil! Daemon! Just leave me alone.'

How could I convince her that it really was me? What could I say that would prove it beyond doubt? Before I could think of anything, Alice began to scream as if she was in terrible pain.

'Please, stop hurting me. Stop it! Stop it! I can't stand any more. Oh please, don't do that!'

She stopped begging then, but started crying and moaning as if in great pain.

'Have you heard enough, Tom?' the Fiend asked me. 'It won't be long before you share her torment. And what she is suffering is far worse than that of a witch being tested. Think of the jabbing of sharp pins; imagine the weight of heavy rocks constricting the chest; feel the flames of the fire flickering nearer and nearer to the stake. The flesh bubbles and the blood boils. It hurts so much, but eventually death brings release. For Alice, though, there is no such respite. She is trapped in the dark for eternal torment. Eternal! That means it will go on *for ever*! And soon I'll be back to collect you. The power of the jar has almost failed.'

I sensed the Fiend move away from me, and Alice's cries gradually faded away until I was left in silence once again. I was shaking with emotion. I could do nothing to help Alice in any way; it was more than I could bear.

Gradually things returned to normal: the cries of the street traders could be heard outside and the attic grew steadily lighter. I struggled to my feet and, driven almost mad by what I'd heard, staggered from wall to wall until I collapsed and lost consciousness again.

The next thing I knew, Thin Shaun was shaking me by the shoulder.

I was sitting up, my back against the wall by the door. On the floor beside me was a bowl of a dark, steaming liquid and a spoon. Shaun dipped the spoon into it and brought it slowly towards my mouth. I tried to twist away but he held my head with his free hand and pushed the spoon hard against my lips. Much of the hot liquid was spilled, but I realized that there was no spicy tang – it wasn't the poisoned gruel. It tasted like oxtail soup.

'There's nothing in this to harm you,' Thin Shaun told me. 'It's nourishment' – he smiled evilly – 'to keep you alive for a little while longer.'

I wasn't sure whether to believe him or not, but I was too weak and weary to resist, and I allowed him to feed me the bowl of soup until it was all gone.

Shaun unlocked the door and carried me out of the attic, once more slung over his shoulder like a sack of potatoes. By now it was dusk, and the square was deserted except for a group of cloaked figures gathered around a tall wooden structure set at the highest point of the sloping triangular marketplace. I realized that they'd rebuilt the wooden tower.

Next to the structure stood a large block of stone with a strange curved depression in its top. I had seen one before in the village of Topley, close to the farm where I was born. They hadn't used that stone for over a hundred years, but nobody had forgotten its purpose. It was an execution block. The victim rested his head on the stone before the executioner chopped it off.

Thin Shaun dumped me on my feet and I stood there, swaying. A hand gripped my arm to steady me, and I looked into the eyes of the witch. 'Say hello to your new friend!' she mocked. 'You are both in for a nasty surprise.'

In her other hand she held the collar of a huge goat. In front of its horns, a bronze crown had been lashed to its head with barbed wire, which was spattered with the creature's blood.

'Meet King Puck!' Scarabek continued. 'You two are going to share the platform, and the madness and pain that accompany that honour. Before this night is done we will summon Pan.'

The goat was led onto the wooden boards and tethered by silver chains bound tightly about its hind legs and fastened to iron rings. That way the animal was confined and could be raised aloft. I was pushed down onto the platform, forced to kneel beside the goat, and blindfolded, my hands still tied behind my back. The wooden planks began to creak and groan as, using a system of ropes and pulleys, four men began to haul us slowly upwards. Once the platform had reached the top of its wooden shaft, they lashed the ropes into position so as to keep us there.

The goat began to bleat and struggle, but it couldn't free itself. I sat up and somehow wriggled my head and shoulders to dislodge the blindfold. I took stock of my surroundings. As far as I could see, no guards had been left to keep an eye on me. I gazed down on the cobbled marketplace and the surrounding rooftops. In the distance I could just about make out the bridge across the river. The spook in me began to assess my chances of escaping.

And darkness was falling rapidly now. Apart from the mages and their supporters, the town seemed deserted. No doubt the people were all hiding behind locked and barred doors. Below, I heard the chanting begin, and a chill suddenly ran up and down my spine.

The mages had begun the summoning.

The initial chants seemed to have no effect, but I noticed that the breeze first died down, then faded away altogether, and the air became very still. It seemed unnaturally warm too, almost like a balmy midsummer's night.

By now the mages had set out a ring of candles on the cobbles around the base of the hollow wooden tower – I counted thirteen; then they formed a line and circled them slowly in a widdershins direction, their chants gradually becoming louder. The goat, which had been tugging against its chains, bleating desperately, now became quiet and still – so much so that it could have been a statue. But then, after about ten minutes, I noticed that its whole body was quivering. Louder and louder the voices surged, to climax in a shrill scream from the thirteen throats below.

At that point the goat shuddered and emptied its bowels; the slimy mess spread across the wooden boards, some of it dripping down onto the cobbles below. The stink almost made me vomit, and I eased myself right to the edge, grateful that the brown tide had halted just short of me.

When I looked down again, the mages were heading off. I realized that it was impossible to climb down the high wooden tower with my hands bound, so it seemed sensible to conserve my energy. I leaned back against a broad wooden post, drew up my knees and tried to drift off to sleep. But in vain. Under the influence of the poisoned gruel, I'd spent most of the previous two days unconscious, and now I felt wide awake.

So it was that I endured a long, miserable night with the goat on that high platform, trying desperately to think of some way to escape. But I found it hard to focus – my mind kept returning to the same questions. What had happened to my master after we'd escaped from the castle? Had he managed to avoid capture? But uppermost in my mind was my anguish at the loss of Alice. Those thoughts circled in my head endlessly, but the one emotion absent was fear. My own death waited no more than a couple of days in the future, and yet for some reason I wasn't in the slightest bit afraid.

Fear came just before dawn in the faint light of the fading moon.

I suddenly noticed that the goat was staring at me intently. Our eyes met, and for a moment the world began to spin. The goat's face was changing as I watched, stretching and twisting impossibly.

Now I was afraid. Was this transformation taking place because Pan was entering its body? I'd half hoped that the rituals hadn't worked, but now, with a shudder, I realized that the mages might well have been successful. I could end up sharing a platform with an Old God renowned for bringing fear and madness to those he came close to.

Suddenly the goat gave a loud bleat and my moment of terror passed. A cold wind was rising now, blowing in from the northeast, and I began to shiver.

At dawn the mages returned to the square and lowered the platform to the ground. I was dragged off onto the cobbles while, thankfully, someone scrubbed the goat's filth off the wooden boards. My hands were untied, and a bowl of hot soup and two slices of thick bread were thrust at me.

'Don't want you dying on us too soon!' one of the mages said maliciously.

I ate ravenously while the goat was also fed and watered. Surrounded by dozens of watchful eyes, I had no chance of escape. When the empty bowl was taken from me, the mages moved back to allow a huge, shaven-headed man to step forward and confront me. I recognized him immediately.

'Bow your head, boy!' a voice hissed in my ear. 'This is Magister Doolan.'

When I hesitated, my head was seized roughly from behind and forced down. As soon as I was able to straighten my neck again, I looked up into the face of the most powerful of the goat mages, the one they called the Bantry Butcher. When his eyes met mine, I saw that they were indeed the eyes of a fanatic: they gleamed with certainty. Here was a man with an inflexible mind who would do anything to further his cause.

'You are here to suffer, boy,' he said, raising his voice so that the assembled mages could hear his every word. 'Your suffering is our gift to Scarabek, in thanks for her generosity in giving her life for our cause. The life of a spook's apprentice should be a most welcome addition to our sacrifices. It will also serve as a lesson to any who might think to oppose us.'

He pointed to the executioner's block and smiled coldly; then my hands were tied once more and I was hoisted aloft.

Within the hour the triangular patch of cobbles was full of stalls. Cattle were driven through the streets to holding pens. As the day progressed, people gradually became more boisterous, sitting in doorways or lounging against walls, tankards of ale in their hands. This was the first morning of the three-day fair, and the inhabitants of Killorglin – along with those who had travelled many miles to be here – were starting to enjoy the festivities.

By the time the sun set behind the houses, the marketplace was empty again. The platform was lowered and I was dragged off onto the cobbled area. Magister Doolan was waiting with his huge double-bladed axe. Now he was dressed in black like an executioner, with leather gloves and a long leather butcher's apron. But there were leather straps crisscrossing his body: these held knives and other metal implements, and I was reminded of Grimalkin, the witch assassin, who carried her weapons in a similar manner. He turned and looked me up and down as if estimating the size of coffin I'd need, and then gave me an evil grin.

For a terrifying moment I thought I was going to be executed there and then. But I was mistaken. There was no sign of the witch, but standing next to the executioner was Cormac, the mage whom we had interrogated. It seemed that the moment of his death had now arrived. The candles were lit, and the mages were gathered around the execution stone.

Cormac knelt and placed his neck in the hollow of the stone. Below his head a metal bucket waited. Someone brought the goat to stand beside the bucket. To my surprise, it thrust out its tongue and licked the mage's left cheek three times, then bleated softly. At that, the other mages nodded and smiled. They seemed to be congratulating themselves. Apparently the ritual was going well.

Doolan opened the collar of Cormac's shirt so as to expose his neck. Then he raised the double-bladed axe. One of the watching mages started to blow into a small musical instrument. It consisted of five thin metal cylinders bound into a row. The sound was thin and reed-like, and it reminded me of the wind sighing through the rushes at a lake edge. The sound was melancholic – it was filled with the sadness of loss and the inevitability of death.

The mages began to chant in unison; a sing-song lament. All at once both the voices and the pipes became silent and I saw the axe come down in a fast arc. I closed my eyes and heard the metal blade strike stone; then something fell heavily into the bucket. When I looked again, Doolan was holding Cormac's head by its hair and shaking it over the goat so that the severed neck sprayed it with drops of blood. Soon the goat – presumably under some dark magic spell – was greedily lapping the blood of the dead man from the bucket.

Five minutes later they were ready to haul the platform up again. They didn't bother to feed me this time. I wasn't hungry anyway: I felt sickened by what I'd witnessed. However, they did hold a cup of water to my lips and I managed four or five gulps.

Aloft once more, I watched the mages: the procedure was exactly the same as on the previous night. Round and round the candles they went, against the clock. This time, when the chants reached a shrill climax, the goat merely turned its head and looked straight at me.

Can a goat smirk? All I can say is that it seemed to be mocking me, and a chill went right down my spine. I was now certain that the ritual was working. At any moment Pan would enter the body of the goat and I would be sitting on this small platform next to him, facing madness and terror.

The night seemed endless. The mages had gone, and a wind was now shrieking across the rooftops, driving squalls of cold rain in my face. I turned my back on it, bowed my head and tossed it forward repeatedly until my hood dropped over my hair. Then I hunkered down, attempting to shelter from the elements as best I could. But it was useless, and soon I was soaked to the skin. The goat began to bleat, louder and louder; after a while it seemed to me that it was even calling my name, then laughing insanely. With my hands tied, I couldn't push my fingers into my ears to blot out the noise.

Finally the sky grew lighter, and within hours the market was full of people once more.

It was growing dark again and the rain had eased by the time the platform was lowered and I stepped onto the cobbles. I was shaking with cold. I was really hungry by now and glad of the plate of mutton and dry bread my captors gave me, once my hands had been untied. I wolfed the whole lot down.

My instincts told me that something was about to happen. Was it the witch's turn to be sacrificed? My stomach knotted with nerves at that thought. Before she died, she'd no doubt want to have her revenge in full. But if I was indeed to be executed now, why had they bothered to feed me? Time ticked by. The mages were growing agitated. And then Doolan arrived, axe over his shoulder.

'Scarabek has vanished,' he growled. 'I find it hard to believe that she should let us down like this.'

'What about the barrow keeper, sir?' one of the mages asked.

'There's no sign of him either, but we can't fail now!'

the Butcher cried. 'Not when things have gone so well. Two sacrifices have already been made.' He turned towards me and stared with hard cruel eyes. 'We'll execute the boy first to make it three. It could buy us some time by appeasing Pan until Scarabek returns.'

There was a murmur of approval, and Doolan began to pull on his gloves. Rough hands seized me and I was dragged towards the execution block.

CHAPTER 12
THE OLD GOD, PAN

There were simply too many of them – I had no hope of resisting their combined strength. The mages pushed me down onto my knees, and seconds later my throat was positioned against the cold damp stone.

I began to shake. Even stronger than my fear of the axe was the knowledge that at the moment of my death I would immediately be snatched away by the Fiend. I struggled again, but someone was holding my hair, keeping my head down, my neck exposed, ready for the axe; my outstretched arms were pulled so tight that they were in danger of being torn from their sockets. I was helpless.

I sensed the axe being raised, and tensed myself for the inevitable blow, squeezing my eyelids shut. Everything was over. I thought of the Spook. I had failed him. Then, at the very last moment, I heard footsteps coming towards us.

'Wait!' shouted a voice that I immediately recognized. It was Thin Shaun, the barrow keeper.

'Where is Scarabek?' the Butcher demanded.

'She'll bring her head to the block willingly, don't you worry,' Thin Shaun told him. 'I'll lay my life on it. Why kill the boy now? She hasn't finished with him yet. There is still tomorrow. I guarantee she will be here by then.'

'Then, once again, I ask you: where is she now?'

'She is a prisoner, but I will follow and release her. She hasn't been taken far—'

'Our enemies have her – the Alliance?'

'Enemies have her, yes, but not ones that are known to us,' Shaun answered. 'They must certainly be powerful to have taken her unawares. But they'll regret this. They have yet to face my wrath. I am the keeper of the barrows. Then they'll wish they'd never been born!'

Although he spoke of 'wrath', Thin Shaun seemed very calm, displaying little emotion. I wondered if he was really human at all.

I was hauled to my feet and stood there, trembling, while the mages walked away to discuss Shaun's news. Two of their servants still gripped my arms. In any case, I was too weak to run away.

Doolan returned and addressed Thin Shaun. 'You have until the same time tomorrow night, when we'll perform the fourth and final rite – otherwise we'll kill the boy in her place. For our efforts to be successful, it is vital that Scarabek is here to offer herself voluntarily.'

Shaun nodded and left immediately. My hands were tied again, and I was dragged onto the platform next to the goat. It was rapidly hoisted into the air and I knelt there in shock. I had come within seconds of death; I had sensed the axe beginning to fall.

Once I'd collected my senses I started thinking about what Thin Shaun had said. *Who* could have snatched Scarabek? She was powerful – not easy to overcome.

Maybe it was the Spook? After all, Shaun had claimed that someone 'unknown' had done it. If so, my master would now be in grave danger.

The night passed very slowly, and long before dawn the goat began to bleat pitifully, as if in pain. In the pale moonlight, I saw drops of blood ooze from the wounds on its head, where the barbed wire had cut it. The blood ran in rivulets down its face, circling its eyes to reach its mouth, whereupon its tongue emerged and began to lick it away.

Now the goat's cries changed dramatically; they became powerful, as if sending out a challenge. I wanted to avert my gaze but was unable to do so: I was forced to watch as the goat's face began to distort and change into something half human, half animal.

Dread came then – a feeling of terror of something loathsome and terrible – but it was different from that cast by any witch. I had faced those spells before, and usually knew how to overcome their effects. But this had something else, an added ingredient: a touch of *compulsion* too. I felt a sudden urge to move close to the goat, a need to touch it. Unable to help myself, I shuffled forward on my knees until I was so close that the fetid breath of the creature washed over me.

The goat was now fully transformed. I was in the presence of Pan. He had a human face with a hint of the bestial; wild and rugged, ravaged by the elements. The horns had gone but the hooves remained; the only other remaining animal feature was the eyes: the pupils were black slits that glittered insanely.

Pan lurched from all fours to stand upright, towering over me, his hind hooves still bound by the silver chains. And then he laughed long and loud – with the uncontrollable, delirious hilarity of the insane. Wasn't he reputed to drive his victims mad? I felt completely lucid; my thoughts seemed ordered and logical. I was afraid, yes, and took deep breaths to calm myself, but for now it appeared that he was the crazy one, not me.

Did being a spook's apprentice help me to remain relatively rational? No sooner had that thought entered my head than everything began to spin and I was plunged into utter darkness. I felt myself falling anyway. It was as if the wooden structure had collapsed beneath me and I was hurtling down towards the cold cobbles below.

I heard the wind whistling through reeds, and water trickling musically across rocks nearby. I was lying on my back; I immediately opened my eyes and sat up; the first thing I noticed was that my hands were no longer bound.

I was sitting on a grassy bank close to a river, which was gleaming like silver. I looked up, expecting to see the moon, but the sky was dark. Then I noticed that *everything* around me was glowing with a faint silvery light. At the river margin, tall reeds swayed rhythmically in the light wind that was blowing downstream towards me. They too gave off that silver sheen.

Where was I? How was this possible? Was it a dream? If so, it had an unusual clarity to it: I could smell blossoms on the breeze, and the ground felt very solid beneath me. To my left was the edge of a forest, which continued on the other bank. There were deciduous trees as far as the eye could see, the branches heavy with blooms, and the air was balmy. It seemed to be high summer, not the chill pre-spring weather of Killorglin.

I got to my feet and heard a new sound. At first I thought it was the whistle of the wind ruffling the reeds, but there were definite notes and I found it compelling. I wanted to hear more.

So I set off upstream towards the sound. I came to a wide grassy clearing that edged the river, where I saw an astonishing sight. It was full of hundreds of animals – mostly rabbits and hares, but there were a few foxes and a couple of badgers, all staring towards the source of the music, their eyes wide and unblinking as if they'd been hypnotized. Additionally, the trees all around were full of birds of many types.

A young boy was sitting on a rock playing a pipe. It appeared to be made from a simple reed, but the music he created was exquisite. His hair was long, his face very pale, and he was clothed in a garment that seemed to be fashioned out of leaves and grass. The face was fully human, but for his ears, which were elongated and a little pointy. His feet were bare, and his toenails were so long that each curled up into a spiral.

From my reading of the Spook's Bestiary I knew that this must be Pan. This was his least threatening shape. In the form of a boy the god was sometimes considered benign, the life force of nature itself.

The boy looked up at me and stopped playing. Immediately the creatures of the forest fled, the spell of the music broken. In a few seconds there were only the two of us left.

'Where am I?' I asked. I felt very calm and not in the least afraid.

'Does it matter where you are?' the boy said. He smiled pleasantly but his next words filled me with sudden terror. 'I've brought you to the region where I dwell. This is what you call the "dark", the place you fear the most!'

CHAPTER 13
A PACT

I looked up at the trees, which still shimmered with silver light. Could this *really* be the dark? I wondered. It certainly wasn't what I'd anticipated. But Pan was right. This had been my biggest fear of all – to be dragged off to the dark after my death. But I had expected the Fiend to do that.

'I didn't expect the dark to be like this,' I said, my voice hardly more than a whisper.

'That's because it isn't the dark,' Pan replied sweetly.

'But you just said it was . . .'

'Listen to me carefully, boy. I said it's a place that you *call* the dark. In truth, this is a shadow world that lies between Limbo and the dark itself. It is a resting place.

To me it is the Hollow Hills, but is called Tech Duinn by the people of Ireland – or sometimes the Otherworld. Their gods like this place – as do their dead heroes. But most humans can't stay here for long – their memories bleed away into the silver light and they are lost for ever. Only heroes can endure. But you needn't fear that now, because only your soul is here. Your body is back on the platform with that reeking animal.'

'The Morrigan? Is she here too?' I asked, glancing nervously up into the trees.

'She comes here on occasion, but not just now.'

'Am I dead?' I wanted to know.

'Not yet,' Pan replied, 'but if you stay here too long, you certainly will be. Your body is barely breathing. You need to return as quickly as possible, so let's not waste any time. I brought you here so that we could talk. It took all my strength: I keep being drawn back into the body of the goat, and it's getting harder to resist the mages' dark magic. Being in your world drives me insane – then I infect others with that same madness.'

'What do you want to talk about?' I asked. Was he actually going to return me to the world again?

'I need you to do something for me. In return, you get to keep your sanity.'

I nodded cautiously. What could one of the Old Gods want of me? What could I do that he couldn't manage himself?

'All you have to do is release the hooves of the goat from the silver chains that bind them.'

'How can I do that? My hands are tied,' I reminded him.

'You'll think of something – I'm certain of that,' Pan said with a smile. 'Then, once you have freed me, I will do the rest.'

'The rest? What will you do then?'

'I will leave the goat's body and escape the control of the mages. To be summoned in that way is abhorrent to me.'

'I thought that the Old Gods wanted to be wor-shipped . . .' I said.

'The mages don't truly worship me – not

respectfully; they just use me to their own advantage. Employing those arcane rituals, they force me into the body of the goat and draw forth my power bit by bit. It weakens me and strengthens them.'

'Have they gained power already?' I asked.

'Some – their dark magic will be strong for a while,' he told me.

'I'll do my best,' I agreed. 'But there's something else that I'd like from you . . .'

Pan raised his eyebrows.

'I have a friend called Alice, who was brought alive into the dark. Could you find her for me and release her too?'

'Who brought her here?'

'The Fiend,' I replied.

'Then it's hopeless,' said the god. 'In the dark there are many different domains. I have one there too. Each being has his own domain, which is generated by his power. The Fiend is a law unto himself and owns the largest domain of all. It is a terrible place for a mortal to be, living or dead. If I could, I would help. But I am powerless. We must go back now. I'm not strong enough to keep us both here for much longer.'

I nodded, and Pan began to play his pipe again. All around us there was a rustling and a beating of wings as the creatures entered the clearing, summoned by his compelling music.

Suddenly the sound of pipes ceased; everything began to fade, and my sight darkened once more.

I found myself lying on the platform. I struggled up into a sitting position and looked down onto the marketplace to be sure that no one was watching. I stared at the goat. It gave a bleat, so I turned my back on it and thrust my hands towards its mouth. I had thought of a way to release my bonds.

The goat sniffed at the rope, and then began to chew with relish. Once or twice it nipped my skin and I flinched away, but it took the animal only a few minutes to release me.

I rubbed my hands to restore the circulation; then I turned my attention to the problem of freeing the goat.

The silver chains that tethered it were designed to hold captive a being from the dark as well as an earthly animal. There was no way that I could force the links apart with my bare hands. In my possession was the special key that could open most locks. Never knowing when I might need it again, I decided that although it might just be possible to use it to break a link, it wasn't worth damaging it unless I had to.

I turned my attention to the fastenings that secured the chains to the wooden boards. The moon was bright, and I was able to see the situation clearly. The wood itself was new and strong, and there was no way I could pull them free. But then I saw that the chain was attached to two small iron rings, which were fastened to the wood by screws. Could I undo them? The mages had evidently never imagined that anyone would try. Maybe they hadn't tightened them very hard?

I thought for a moment, before searching in my pocket again and finding a coin. I inserted the edge into the head of the screw and turned. It wouldn't budge. I pressed down as hard as I could; finally it began to move. Soon I was removing the screw with just my fingers.

The second screw proved much more difficult. I almost despaired of moving it, and the groove in the head of the screw started to shear away, but at last it turned. Eventually the iron ring came away from the boards, and the goat was free.

The creature looked at me and bleated once. It seemed to tense its body; then, to my astonishment, it leaped off the platform.

I watched, horrified, as the goat plunged towards the ground and hit the cobbles with a dull thump. It didn't cry out on impact, but its legs twitched a few times and a puddle of blood began to form beneath it. The crown fell off its head and rolled away across the marketplace. Now I realized that it was through the goat's death that Pan had intended to free himself.

The god didn't leave our world quietly: a howling gale sprang up from nowhere, which blew out all the windows facing the marketplace and hurled tiles from the roofs down to smash on the cobbles. Doors blew off their hinges, and shouts rent the night air.

Fearing that it might topple over at any moment, I began to climb down from the platform, my feet seeking out the struts of the wooden shaft. I needn't have worried – the wind was directed at the mages, who'd taken rooms facing the market; the tower, right in the calm eye of the storm, barely moved.

Moonlight lit up the whole area, giving me no place to hide, and by the time I reached the ground I could see mages heading towards the wooden structure. One gave a cry of anguish as he reached the body of the goat. I started sprinting down the triangle towards the street at the bottom, but someone holding a long-bladed, curved knife blocked my path. I swerved around him and headed for the river, which lay like a silver ribbon in the distance. There were trees beyond it; dark, shadowy areas. Once across the bridge, I'd have a good chance of escaping.

I glanced back and saw that I was being followed. I tried to hurry, but my body didn't respond, still weak after spending long days and nights on the platform, exposed to the elements and eating little. When I looked back again, my pursuers were catching up fast. But I was approaching the bridge now. There was still just a slim chance that I could cross it and escape into the trees.

That hope was short-lived. I heard the sound of galloping hooves and knew that I was just moments from recapture or death. The first rider came at me from the right. I saw the glint of a sword in the moonlight, and ducked to my left as it swept down towards my head. Whether the blow was intended to kill me or he'd just been using the flat of his sword, I couldn't tell, but other horsemen quickly surrounded me, pointing their weapons at me, waiting until the runners caught up.

Moments later rough hands seized me, and I was dragged back up the slope towards the marketplace. Magister Doolan was waiting beside the tower, grim-faced.

'You have a lot to answer for, boy!' he said, cuffing me twice about the head, making my ears sing. 'I'd love to slice you up slowly myself, but I'll give you to the witch. She'll know best how to make you suffer.'

With that, my hands and feet were tied and I was thrown over the back of a horse. All around me I heard a bustle as the mages and their followers prepared to leave Killorglin. Soon we were off, heading south in a long convoy. No doubt the mages feared that the Alliance would take this opportunity to attack, and we hurried along so quickly that those on foot had to jog to keep up with the horses.

I'd had a brief taste of freedom. Now it seemed that we were bound for the refuge of the mages, the Staigue ring fort. According to Shey, its defences were impregnable. Once inside, I'd be as good as dead. They'd hand me over to the witch.

Despite everything, I allowed myself the small satisfaction of reflecting that the mages had been forced to abandon their ceremony.

It had failed, and I had been the one to stop it.

CHAPTER
~14~
THE HEAD OF THE WITCH

By dawn we were deep in the southern hills. It was now raining hard and I was soaked to the skin. I hung face down against the horse's flank, bouncing up and down uncomfortably, so my main view was of the boggy ground.

My first glimpse of the Staigue fort came when I was dragged off the horse and my feet were freed. I looked up at what appeared to be a gigantic dry-stone wall towering over us, the stones skilfully positioned one upon the other, without the use of mud or mortar to bind them together. The 'ring fort' was a good name for it, because that's exactly what it was – a huge defensive circle of stones. Everyone was dismounting, and I soon found out why. The fort could only be entered by a very narrow gate, which was far too small for a horse.

Once through that gap in the wall, I got my first sight of the inside of the mages' fortification. It had no roof, but the walls were very high, with nine separate flights of stone steps leading up to ramparts, from which attackers could be repelled. The ground within it was churned to soft mud, but dotted about were a number of timber buildings. The stone fort was clearly very old, but these wooden constructions looked relatively recent. Some appeared to be dwellings, but the central one, which was round in shape, probably had a different purpose; it was towards this building that I was dragged.

We didn't enter right away. I was forced to sit down in the mud and surrounded by four guards armed with swords. While we waited, the narrow gap through which we'd entered the fort was sealed with stones. The job was done so expertly that there was no sign at all of where the entrance had been. I assumed that someone had remained outside to take the horses away to shelter.

At last I was hauled to my feet and the Butcher led the way into the large building. Inside stood a circular, elevated dais. It was stained and polished, and marked upon its surface was a large pentacle of the type mages used to summon a daemon or other supernatural entity. A number of chairs and a table were set out at the centre. Around the dais, the floor was mud, and there must have been at least nine armed guards standing up to their ankles in it. Upon the dais stood seven barefoot mages, and near its edge was Thin Shaun. He was cradling his son, Konal, who was still wrapped in a blanket. Shaun's hood was pulled forward, his head bowed and in shadow.

Doolan approached the edge of the wooden structure to address him. 'Where is Scarabek?' he snapped.

'I failed – despite my best efforts she is still a prisoner. But her enemy is prepared to exchange her for the boy. I advise you to let him go' – Shaun nodded at me – 'then you'll have Scarabek to sacrifice next time we attempt the ritual.'

'*Who* is this enemy?' demanded the chief mage angrily.

Thin Shaun lifted his head, and with his left hand pulled back his hood so that his face was visible. Even before he spoke I knew the identity of the enemy who had bested him. Her sign was carved into his forehead and it was still weeping blood.

'Her name is Grimalkin – she's an assassin, and has come from a powerful witch clan over the water. Never have I encountered someone with such skill. All my strength and magic proved useless against her. I was completely at her mercy,' Shaun admitted.

Suddenly I was filled with new hope. Grimalkin was here!

'Is she alone,' demanded Doolan, 'or supported by other clan members?'

'She is alone.'

'Then she can be dealt with.'

Shaun looked away.

'Although we failed to raise the god, the attempt did bear some fruit . . .' The Butcher's voice was full with confidence. 'It has made our magic stronger. She is only one; if we fill a mage with our combined strength, just one of our number will be enough to kill her. I will be her executioner!'

Doolan bowed his head and started to mutter to himself; the words he spoke were in the Old Tongue – he was using dark magic. As he did so, the seven other mages knelt in a huddle at the edge of the dais and chanted for a minute or so before suddenly falling silent.

Then they moved close to Doolan and stretched out their arms, laying their hands on his head, shoulders, upper back and chest. They began to chant again, and in response, the man they called the Butcher closed his eyes and began to shudder.

I remembered how they had performed a similar ritual with the gunners at the siege of Ballycarbery

Castle. Before the mages had invested them with power, they had been ineffectual; afterwards, they had become devastatingly accurate and had breached the castle wall. Doolan was formidable already. How much more dangerous would he become? Could he pose a real threat to Grimalkin?

At last the mages fell silent and withdrew their hands. 'I go now!' the Butcher told them, showing his teeth. 'I'll bring back the head of our enemy!'

He left the hall, and I was dragged out after him. I wondered how he was going to leave the fort. Surely they wouldn't have to remove the stones that now blocked the entrance? The mage headed for the nearest set of steps that led up to the ramparts at the top of the wall. Beside them stood an iron pillar. Fastened to it and coiled beneath it was a long length of strong rope. He seized the end and dragged the rope after him as he ascended. I watched him throw it down outside the wall. Then he clambered across the top and disappeared from view. He was climbing down the rope to reach the ground.

After a few moments he gave a shout, and one of the guards ran to the pillar and began to haul on the rope. The end appeared over the wall and slithered down the steps like a snake. At that point I was forced to squat in the wet mud again. Then we waited.

We waited all day; nothing happened. They changed my guard twice. I was wet through again, shivering from the cold and damp and close to starvation.

Then, at dusk, I heard a distant cry. It sounded like something in great pain.

One of the guards spat in the mud. 'Just an animal,' he said. However, my experience as an apprentice spook told me that it was more likely to be human.

From time to time a mage climbed the ramparts and peered out into the night. By now, even allowing for the elevation of the land, the moon should have been visible to the east. But the thick clouds promised more rain, and the night grew darker. Lanterns were hung from hooks on the wall, but for some reason the light they cast was weak, as if the darkness itself was viscous and thick. I could hear the voices of the mages, but they were muffled and indistinct.

Then a voice called loudly and clearly from beyond the wall. 'Lower the rope!'

I recognized that deep gruff voice. It was the Butcher. Had he been successful? I wondered.

A guard threw the end of the rope down, and moments later Doolan was standing on the ramparts; the soldier held a lantern close to his face. Doolan led the way down the steps again. When he reached the mud at the bottom and approached the first wall-lantern, I realized that he was carrying something in his left hand. By now Thin Shaun had emerged from the round hut, half a dozen mages following close behind.

They waited behind me as Doolan strode through the mud. With his right hand he drew a long blood-stained knife from his belt; in his left, casually held by the hair, was a severed head. I felt sick to the pit of my stomach. The Butcher raised it up so that the mages could get a good look at it.

I recognized that face – both beautiful and cruel, with

high cheekbones and lips that were painted black.

'Behold! The head of the witch!' he cried.

I was looking at the face of the witch assassin.

Grimalkin was dead.

CHAPTER 15
DARK ANGEL

My heart sank into my boots. Everything was lost. My hope of escape had been snatched away. Grimalkin had also offered our only real hope of binding the Fiend. I felt sad too. She had been a malevolent witch, the assassin of the Malkin clan, but we had fought alongside each other. Without Grimalkin's help, I would be dead already.

'Where is Scarabek?' asked Thin Shaun.

'She's safe enough,' Doolan told him, 'but was hurt in the struggle. I came on ahead to bring you the news. She is happy for me to deal with the boy and give him the slow death he justly deserves. I will start now,' he said, lifting the knife and licking the blood from its long blade.

I was pulled to my feet and my bonds were cut. Then Shaun seized me by the hair and dragged me towards the chief mage.

'Death has come for you, boy!' he cried. 'Look upon his fearsome face!'

The Butcher, Doolan, smiled grimly. Then he said something very strange:

'Death has sent his dark angel instead!'

Dark angel? What did he mean?

I looked at Doolan and saw that there was something weird about him. A purple light shimmered around his head, and his face seemed to be melting. He was shifting his shape. His lips were now black. The forehead seemed narrower too; the cheekbones higher. It was no longer the face of the chief mage.

It was Grimalkin.

As usual, the witch assassin was dressed to deal out death: her body was criss-crossed with leather straps, each holding more than one sheath; they housed her blades, and the scissors she used to snip away the thumb-bones of her defeated enemies. From her left shoulder was suspended a small hessian sack. What new weapon did that contain? I wondered. Her lips were painted black, and when she opened her mouth I could see those terrifying teeth, each one filed to a sharp point. She looked dangerous; every inch a killer.

The witch assassin had used a cloak of dark magic to deceive her enemies. I felt a surge of joy: I wasn't dead yet. In her left hand Grimalkin held the severed head of Doolan, which she now tossed disdainfully into the mud at her feet. In one fluid motion she hurled the long knife towards me with terrible force. But I was not the target, and Grimalkin rarely missed.

Thin Shaun screamed, and his hand convulsed before releasing my hair. I turned and watched him fall to his knees in the mud, the knife up to its hilt in his chest. The mages around me panicked and started to move backwards, away from the witch.

Grimalkin ran forward, grabbed me by the left shoulder and spun me behind her. I slipped and went down on my hands and knees in the mud. Now she was between me and our enemies, crouching, ready to attack. A guard launched a spear towards her chest. The aim was good and it was fast, but at the last moment she knocked it aside with the edge of her hand, simultaneously hurling another knife. The guard died even before his spear had been deflected to the ground. I scrambled to my feet.

'Run for the steps! Use the rope!' the witch cried, pointing towards the wall.

I did as she commanded, but I was unfit after long days and nights of imprisonment and ill-treatment. My legs felt sluggish, the mud sucking at my boots and delaying my progress. I glanced back and saw that, as yet, Grimalkin was making no attempt to follow me. She was fighting a dozen mages and guards, whirling and cutting. I heard screams and groans of agony as her blades slashed and stabbed, driving back her foes.

I'd reached the steps; I began to climb as fast as I was able, my legs as heavy as lead. I was now at the ramparts and glanced back down again. Grimalkin had retreated, and was fighting next to the iron pillar to which the end of the rope was tied.

I suddenly saw a great danger. Once she left that position and tried to make her own escape, they would cut through the rope. Surely she must be aware of the danger, I thought. I clambered over the edge of the wall and began to climb down. I felt dizzy and spun round and round on the rope, finding it hard to hold on.

At last, breathless and weak with exertion, I reached the ground and looked up. There were cries from beyond the ramparts; then Grimalkin appeared at the top of the wall and began her rapid descent. My heart was in my mouth, but she was suddenly there at my side, pointing to the east.

'Our best hope is to follow the coast that way!' she told me.

Without waiting for a reply, she ran off; I kept up as best I could, but she began to get further and further ahead. She halted and came back towards me. Turning, I could see the lights of torches on the distance.

'There are too many of them to fight,' she said. 'Soon they'll send for horses as well. You've got to move faster. Our lives depend on it.'

My mind was willing, but my body simply couldn't match its demands. 'I can't,' I said. 'I've been tied up for days and I've eaten little. I'm sorry but I just haven't the strength.'

Without another word, the witch seized me by my legs and heaved me up onto her shoulders as if I were no more than a sack of feathers. Then she headed east.

Grimalkin ran for at least an hour. Once she leaped across a stream; on another occasion she slipped to her knees on a slope. The next thing I knew, I was being taken into some sort of shelter and lowered to the ground. Then I fell into a deep sleep. When I awoke, Grimalkin was cooking something over a fire, the smoke drifting up a chimney.

I sat up slowly and looked about me. It was daylight, and we were sheltering in an abandoned cottage. I could see no furniture, and animals had obviously been using the place before us. There was sheep dung on the stone flags near the doorway. The cottage had no door, and the single window was broken. It was draughty, but the roof was still intact and it was dry.

The witch assassin was crouching in the hearth, slowly rotating two rabbits impaled on spits. She turned and gave me a smile, showing her sharp teeth.

Then, to my surprise, I saw my staff leaning against the wall in the far corner of the room.

'I retrieved your staff from Scarabek's cottage and left it here on my way to Staigue. Are you feeling better now?' she asked.

I nodded. 'Yes, and thank you for saving my life. Again.' I gestured towards the fire. 'Aren't you bothered about the smoke from the chimney? Are they still searching for us?'

'Yes, but they won't find us here – I've cloaked this place with magic. Once night falls we'll continue our journey.'

'Where are we going?' I wondered.

'To Kenmare, to meet your master.'

'Have you spoken to him already?'

'Yes. He made his way back there – though Alice wasn't with him and I've had no further contact with her. She's well beyond the protection of the blood jar.'

I bowed my head. 'The blood jar can't help her now,' I said sadly. 'The Celtic witch, Scarabek, gave Alice to the Fiend, and he took her away into his domain.'

'The poor girl,' Grimalkin replied. 'Then she is lost. There is nothing we can do for her. I wish I'd known that. I let Scarabek go. She'd served her purpose – she was just a way to free you. I should have killed her!'

When I heard these words, I felt a stab of pain in my heart. It confirmed what I already believed about Alice but coming from the witch assassin's lips they held a terrible finality.

'Now that she's free, Scarabek will come looking for me again,' I told her. 'I was with Bill Arkwright when he killed her twin sister. She seeks revenge before giving me to the Fiend.'

'You needn't worry. You'll be safe with me at your side,' Grimalkin said. 'Besides, I took something else from the witch's cottage.'

She handed me the hessian sack I'd noticed earlier. I

opened it and, to my delight, saw that it contained my silver chain.

'Put it away,' Grimalkin said. 'Even lifting it in the sack burned my fingers. I can't bear to be near it!'

Then she held out one of the spits towards me. 'Eat up. You'll need your strength.'

For a while we ate in silence. The rabbit was delicious. I was starving, and kept burning my mouth in my eagerness to wolf it down.

'How did your master take the news about the blood jar?' Grimalkin asked. 'He said little to me; he seemed subdued and deep in thought. He can hardly find it easy to accept that his apprentice is protected by dark magic.'

'He took it very badly,' I answered, automatically checking that it still lay in my pocket. 'For a moment I thought he was going to smash it immediately – sending the three of us to the dark for ever, but then he relented: it was as if your plan had given him new hope. Life's dealt him a bad hand in recent months. His house and library were burned to the ground – the heritage it was his duty to keep safe. He's never been the same since.'

'Well, he won't have expected us to be allies again after Greece. That won't be easy for him either,' she remarked.

'Did Alice tell you that the jar is cracked and starting to fail?'

Grimalkin nodded. 'She did, and it's essential that we deal with the Fiend as soon as possible.'

'How did you escape from Scotland?' I asked.

'By terrifying a poor fisherman into bringing me here,' she replied with a fierce smile. 'I paid him by sparing his life.'

'And how are things back in the County?' I asked, licking the last fragments of succulent rabbit from my fingers.

'At the moment it's very bad. People have nothing – the enemy soldiers have taken everything. But they will not hold sway for ever.'

'But we still might have to wait a long time before venturing home,' I guessed.

I thought of my family, living in the County. How were they surviving the enemy occupation? The farm might well have been raided and the animals driven off to be slaughtered as food for the troops. Would my brothers, Jack and James, have tried to resist? If so, they could be dead.

'The enemy have advanced too far: their forces and their lines of supply are stretched thin,' Grimalkin asserted. 'And they have not yet overcome the most northerly counties. Beyond them, the Lowland Scots are gathering; in the spring they'll be joined by the Highlanders. Then they will launch an attack together, and the men of the County will rise up again – we witches will play our part too. There will be many deaths. We will drive the enemy south, then into the sea. Our scryers have seen it come to pass.'

Witch scryers really *did* see the future, but I knew that they could also be wrong, so I didn't comment. Instead, I directed Grimalkin's thoughts towards our most powerful enemy. 'Do you really believe that we can bind the Fiend?' I asked.

'Would I have come all this way otherwise?' She gave me a brief smile. 'Though we need to discuss everything with John Gregory. The attempt will be dangerous and could be the end of us. It's a big risk – but, yes, I do believe that it can be done. Where the Fiend is bound is important. It must be possible to hide the site from those who might wish to release him.'

'By dark magic?'

The witch assassin nodded. 'Yes, I will wrap a cloak of dark magic about the place. But it must be remote – we cannot have anyone stumbling upon it by chance.'

After dark we continued towards Kenmare. I was feeling much stronger now, and was pleased to feel my staff in my hand and the familiar chink of my silver chain in my pocket. Mostly we strode along in silence, but I was preoccupied by thoughts of Alice's plight, and eventually I brought the subject up again.

'Is there really no hope for Alice?' I asked. 'No way of getting her back?'

'I fear we can do nothing. I wish it were otherwise.'

'But what if we do manage to bind the Fiend? Won't that make a difference?'

'When we destroy the blood jar, he will come, desperate to seize you. He will leave Alice behind, and there she will remain. I know it is a terrible thing to accept – but console yourself with the thought that, once he's been bound and cut off from his domain, Alice's pain will surely lessen. He will not be there to mete it out.'

Grimalkin's attempt to console me failed. I thought of Alice, trapped in the dark, lonely, afraid and in unimaginable torment. I remembered the words of Pan . . .

The Fiend is a law unto himself and owns the largest domain of all. It is a terrible place for a mortal to be, living or dead.

CHAPTER
~16~
THE DRAGON'S LAIR

We reached Kenmare about two hours before dawn, and approached the high wall that enclosed Shey's fortified mansion. Intercepted by several aggressive guards at the gate, Grimalkin drew a blade and showed them her pointed teeth. In the lantern-light she looked every inch the fearsome witch, but the men, although they recognized me, were wary of a witch and prepared to attack.

There were five of them, but I wouldn't have given much for their chances against Grimalkin. However, sense prevailed, and I persuaded them to send one of their number back to the house to wake Shey and the Spook. The guard returned quickly, muttered an apology, and we were escorted in.

I had a brief meeting alone with my master and told him what had happened. When I came to the part where the Fiend had disappeared, taking the terrified Alice back into the dark with him, a lump came into my throat and I gave a sob, my eyes filling with tears.

The Spook put his hand on my shoulder and patted it gently. 'There's little I can say to make you feel better, lad. Just try to be strong.'

Grimalkin and I joined the Spook and Shey in the study in the east wing, where a peat fire was burning in the hearth.

I suppose I'd never expected to see the leader of the Land Alliance again, thinking he was bound to be killed when the walls of Ballycarbery Castle were breached. But he told us that the enemy forces had merely come to take the mage we'd held prisoner so that he could be sacrificed. Once that aim was achieved, they'd immediately called off the siege.

'You did well, boy!' Shey congratulated me. 'One of our spies brought us word. Magister Doolan is dead.

Single-handedly, you stopped the ritual. It took some courage to free the goat and push it off the platform.'

'I wasn't really alone,' I told him. Then I explained about my visit to the Hollow Hills and how Pan had played his part.

They all listened in silence, but when I'd finished Shey reached across and clapped me on the back.

'It was incredibly brave,' he said. 'Most people would have been driven insane by him.'

'Indeed, but we're seventh sons of seventh sons,' explained the Spook. 'In such situations that gives us the strength that others lack.'

'Maybe,' said Grimalkin, 'but Tom is more than that. Remember, he also has the blood of his mother running through his veins. Do you really believe that Pan would have deigned to cooperate with *you*, John Gregory, in that way? I think not.'

The Spook didn't reply, but neither did he disagree. Instead, he reached across and picked up Shey's map of Kerry. Then he unfolded it and spread it out on the table.

'Am I right in saying that you've once again reached stalemate with the mages?' he asked, looking directly at the leader of the Land Alliance.

Shey nodded. 'I'm afraid so. The rites may have been brought to a premature end, but they gained some power – any further attack made on them now may be risky.'

'Well, we are going to attempt something very dangerous, but if it succeeds, it could help your cause too,' the Spook went on. 'We are going to try and bind the Fiend – the Devil himself. If that can be achieved, the power of the dark and all its other servants will be reduced. Aye, and that would include the mages.

'What we need is a remote location – a suitable place to bind him. This is your land – where do you suggest?' he asked, pointing at the map.

Shey got to his feet, rested his hands on the table and studied it, tracing the line of the coast southwest towards Cahersiveen with his index finger, before moving inland. 'There's a ruined church here,' he said, jabbing at a point with his finger. 'Kealnagore. The locals think it's haunted, so they stay away. You couldn't choose better than that.'

'It's a little too close to the ring fort at Staigue,' said the Spook. 'The last thing we want is one of the mages coming across it – especially while we're doing the binding.'

Shey moved his finger eastwards and tapped Kenmare. 'Why not do it near here then? This is probably the area that's safest from the interference of the mages. And there is one place that most local folk avoid: a stone circle that lies just outside the village.'

'Is that haunted too?' the Spook asked him.

He shook his head. 'There's something there for sure, but perhaps not a ghost. I visited it once for a wager and felt it myself – though I could see nothing. It's a creepy place, especially after dark. I kept shivering – I just knew that there was something nearby, something huge and terrifying. Even in daylight people keep well away.'

'Well, I suggest that we go and see this haunted stone

circle.' The Spook smiled. 'It could be just what we're looking for!'

It was a bright, clear morning, and the ground was dusted with frost. As yet, there was little warmth in the sun, and our breath steamed up into the crisp air. As the stone circle wasn't far from Shey's house, we set off before breakfast, as soon as it was light. It was perfect weather for walking and we took the dogs. They ran ahead, barking excitedly, glad to be out and reunited with us again.

Soon we could see the stone circle in the distance. It stood on a small hill, surrounded on three sides by trees. On my travels with the Spook I had seen such circles formed with much larger standing stones. Some of the ones here were no more than boulders. I counted twelve of them.

When we reached the circle, the wolfhounds suddenly started to whine; they lay down at its edge and would proceed no further.

I sensed something right away. A cold shiver ran the

length of my spine. Something from the dark was nearby. But to my surprise, my master gave me one of his rare smiles.

'Couldn't be better, lad!' he told me. 'What we have here is a dragon, and a special one to boot! This is a dragon's lair!'

We followed him into the stone circle, Shey looking nervous. Even Grimalkin looked tense, and rested her hand on the hilt of her largest blade. I vaguely remembered reading about such creatures in my master's Bestiary.

'Most people think that a dragon is a huge lizard breathing fire and smoke, but a true dragon is an elemental,' the Spook explained. 'They are air spirits, invisible but immense. This one is probably coiled about within this hill. They live their lives at a different speed to us humans. To them, our lifetimes pass in the blinking of an eye. Most people can barely sense the presence of a dragon, but this one is particularly strong. Can't you feel its malevolence? It's enough to keep people away – and that's exactly what we want.

'However, it wouldn't worry a true servant of the dark,' he continued with a frown, turning to face Shey. 'We can't guarantee that this area will always remain safe and in your hands.'

'I can cloak it,' said Grimalkin. 'Even if the mages camped close to the stones, they would not suspect what was here. Of course, there are other powerful servants of the dark who might see beyond my magic. But first things first . . .'

'Yes, there's no point in delaying. Let's get on with our preparations,' said the Spook. 'We'll try to bind him here, right at the centre of the circle, within the coils of the dragon. Now, I need the services of a stone-mason, and also a good rigger. They must be craftsmen we can trust to keep quiet afterwards. Could you find them for me?' he asked, turning to Shey.

'I know an excellent local stonemason,' he replied. 'The rigger might be more difficult, but I'll make enquiries.'

'And I need something else from you,' said Grimalkin. 'I must fashion spears and nails with which to bind the Fiend. I noticed that you have extensive stables behind your house – do you have a forge?'

'Yes – and an excellent smith who I'll put at your service.'

'The forge itself will suffice. I work alone,' Grimalkin said with a frown. 'I would like to begin the task as soon as possible.'

'Of course – I'll take you there right away,' said Shey nervously, clearly intimidated by the witch.

'Aye,' said the Spook, 'and while you're doing that, the lad and I will get started on the pit.'

Back at the house, after a light breakfast, we collected our bags and a couple of sturdy spades to do the digging. The weather seemed likely to remain fine for the rest of the day. It made sense to get started. It would be no fun at all digging in the rain.

'Well,' said the Spook as I put down our bags and the spades near the centre of the circle of stones, 'this is a good spot. Give me a spade, lad!'

He jabbed it deep into the soft earth and gave a

satisfied grunt. 'The digging should be relatively easy. But first I'll mark out the boundaries of the pit,' he said, taking a folded measuring rod from his bag. 'We'd better make it large – no doubt the Fiend will appear in the same form as he did last time, so it needs to be at least three times as big as a boggart pit. I hope you've recovered your strength after your ordeal, lad.'

That meant there would be a lot of earth to remove. I'd be doing most of the digging, no doubt, even though I still felt weak, and be left with sore muscles and an aching back.

I watched as the Spook marked the dimensions of the pit on the bare earth very precisely, using small wooden pegs and twine. When he'd finished, I picked up the largest spade and set to work. I had a long day ahead of me. Mostly my master just watched, but every hour or so he gave me a break and set to himself.

At first, as I worked, I kept thinking of poor Alice, but after a while my mind went blank and the numbing monotony of hard digging took over. At one point

I paused to catch my breath and leaned heavily on the spade handle.

'What about the stone lid for the pit?' I asked. 'It'll be much heavier than usual and here we have no branch to lower it from.'

When binding boggarts, the rigger usually lashed his block and tackle to a branch and used it to lower the stone. That's why we always dug our pits beneath a large tree.

'The rigger will have to construct a strong wooden gantry, lad, with a beam from which to hang the block. It makes the job more difficult and will take extra time. Not only does the rigger have to be good at his job and able to keep his mouth shut afterwards; he and his mate both need to be brave. Do you remember what happened to poor Billy Bradley?'

Billy had been John Gregory's apprentice before me. The Spook had been ill and was forced to send Billy out alone to bind a dangerous ripper boggart. Things had gone wrong. The stone lid had trapped Billy's fingers, and after finishing the blood in the bait-dish, the ripper had bitten off his fingers. He'd died of shock and loss of blood.

I nodded sadly. 'The riggers panicked,' I recalled.

'That's right, lad. If they'd kept their nerve, that rigger and his mate could have lifted the stone off Billy's fingers in seconds and he'd still be alive today. We need an experienced rigger who doesn't scare easily!'

Suddenly a thought struck me – the carving on the stone . . .

'Where do we leave our mark when the binding is done?' I asked. 'Do we carve a symbol on the top and put our names underneath to show who bound the Fiend himself?'

'It would certainly be the pinnacle of my life's work,' my master replied. 'But we'll leave no mark this time. Nobody must know he's there. We'll put a boulder on top of the stone. That way folks in years to come will just assume it's part of the pattern of standing stones and not think to disturb it.

'Anyway, lad,' he went on. 'You've rested long

enough; let's stop this idle speculation and get back to work! Instead of just cutting out the dimensions of the pit, why don't you test it for depth just about where you're standing now?'

I'd been working methodically, following the marks the Spook had made, keeping the excavation more or less even. But what he said made sense. It was a good tip to put into my notebook for future reference; something that no doubt my master had learned from experience. We had to know if we could achieve the necessary depth. So I started to dig deeper.

I started to feel a chill: was it the dragon sensing me disturbing its lair?

CHAPTER 17
WORDS IN A MIRROR

The following day we soon hit solid rock, and could go no deeper. I hoped the pit would be big enough for our purposes. About mid afternoon, when I'd just about finished, Grimalkin paid us a visit. Over her shoulder she was carrying something wrapped in sacking – no doubt the spears that she'd forged.

'Will that be big enough?' she asked, looking down at the pit doubtfully.

'I hope so. I was going to make it deeper but this rock's put an end to that,' I told her.

Grimalkin looked worried. 'I've seen the Fiend bigger than that. He was a giant, a monster.'

'If he's that big, there may be nothing we can do,' I said.

'Remember, I have given birth to his child – the child he slew,' Grimalkin said. 'He cannot come near me unless I will it. That could be our last line of defence.'

She smiled, curling her lips over her needle-sharp teeth. 'And perhaps that layer of rock will be to our advantage,' she said. 'I have crafted spears and also some shorter nails. The rock will provide a firm base for the binding.'

'Well,' said the Spook, 'we're ready now – as ready as we'll ever be. We can rest now, and gather our strength for the ordeal tonight.'

Grimalkin shook her head. 'No, there is further work to be done first,' she told him. She knelt and unrolled the sacking on the ground to reveal the stakes and nails. I could not see even a hint of silver alloy. They seemed to be crafted of plain steel.

'I need silver to fold into the steel,' she said.

I knew I had no choice. I would have to offer my silver chain. It was a vital tool for a spook, and a

243

present from my mam, but surrendering it would make the binding of the Fiend possible.

'You can use this,' I said, making to hand it to her.

But the Spook frowned. 'Nay, lad, you'll need it again one day. We'll use mine. What better use could it serve? Besides, my old master, Henry Horrocks, had a chain of his own and I inherited it after his death. It's out of harm's way with my brother Andrew in Adlington – at his locksmith's shop. One day, when it's safe to return to the County, we'll go and collect it.'

As he spoke, there was a hint of sadness in the Spook's face. That chain had served him well over the years. To surrender it was hard.

It took nearly two days for Grimalkin to craft the weapons to her satisfaction. Behind the house the forge rang with the rhythmical pounding of her hammer. She melted down my master's silver chain before forming it into strips, which she worked skilfully into the iron of the stakes and the broad-headed nails.

In the afternoon of the second day, one of Shey's

servants brought word that Grimalkin wished to speak to me alone. I entered the shed that housed the forge where she was working. Afraid of disturbing her concentration, I didn't speak, but instead waited patiently in a corner, watching her craft a spear. She wore thick leather gloves to protect her witch's skin from the iron and silver. The long sharp spear in her grasp was being formed into a slender helix, a fine twisting alloy of silver and iron. It was the last of four; the nails had already been completed.

Satisfied at last, she laid the finished weapon down on a bench close to the anvil, and then she turned to face me, her gaze holding mine.

'Listen,' she said, her eyes glittering fiery red with the reflected light of the forge. 'Tonight we'll bind him – whatever it takes. I'd give my life to achieve that, if it was necessary.'

I nodded. 'I fear that the moment the Fiend realizes he's in the pit, he'll halt time. And I won't be strong enough to stop him – though I vow I'll die trying.'

She frowned. 'I have often thought about the Fiend

and his powers. When he's halted time in the past, the initiative has been his. So, rather than being on the defensive and trying to prevent that, why not attack by halting time yourself at the very moment he appears?'

'I've managed to achieve that a couple of times in the past, but the effect hasn't lasted. Still, I'll do my best,' I assured her.

'Succeed, and time will halt for all those in the vicinity of the pit – all but you. The Fiend will quickly understand the situation, but by then you will already have driven your spear deep into his dirty hide.'

I nodded. It might just work. Grimalkin was right. This time I would take the initiative and strike first.

We tried our best to grab a few hours' sleep before dark. We'd need to be strong, rested and alert for the task ahead. I didn't bother getting undressed – though I quickly checked the blood jar in my pocket; the crack still seemed to be holding the Fiend at bay. Then I lay on top of the bedcovers and closed my eyes.

I soon fell into a deep dreamless sleep but, sensing

something strange, I jerked awake, sitting bolt upright.

The mirror on the bedside table was flickering. A face appeared. It was Alice! She was wide-eyed with terror: it wrenched at my heart to see her in that state.

The mirror clouded. She had breathed on the surface of the one she was using. She began to write, and her message slowly appeared.

Help me, Tom!
I can get back with your help!

The letters appeared backwards on the glass: *Help me, Tom! I can get back with your help.*

Could she really escape from the dark? I wondered. All at once I was filled with fresh hope. Quickly I breathed on the mirror and wrote my reply on the misted glass.

How can I help?

Alice began to write again, but the words appeared only very slowly. Was she in pain? What was wrong?

Pan found me a doorway back.
But can't get through alone, can I?
Need your help, Tom.

I read this one with ease, in less time than it had taken her to write it: *Pan found me a doorway back. But can't get through alone, can I? Need your help, Tom.*

Could there really be a doorway back to our world? Pan must be aiding Alice in repayment for my help with the mages. But he'd said he *couldn't* help – that the Fiend was too strong. And how was it possible to use a mirror to communicate from the dark? I wondered. Was that why it was taking her so long to write each message! I quickly breathed on the mirror and wrote again.

Where is the door, Alice?

Her reply came more quickly this time.

Within the lair of the dragon.

The *lair of the dragon*? That was what the Spook had called the circle of stones where we hoped to bind the Fiend.

Do you mean the stone circle at Kenmare?

The mirror flickered and grew dark. My heart plummeted into my boots. Alice had gone before I could get that vital information from her. But just as I began to despair, the mirror filled with light again, and Alice's finger began to write very slowly.

Yes, Kenmare. Come alone.
Pan won't open the door to anyone but you . . .

She was asking me to come alone – that certainly made sense. Grimalkin had told the Spook that Pan had only dealt with me because of my mam. It was dangerous to go alone, but if that was the only way, then I had no choice.

I drew back the curtains and looked through the window. It was twilight; soon it would be completely dark. In the next room I could hear the Spook stirring. From the pouches in my bag I quickly filled my pockets with salt and iron. Next I took my silver chain and tied it around my waist, hiding it under my shirt.

Carrying my boots in one hand and my staff in the other, I tiptoed out through the door, and managed to get downstairs without meeting anyone. One of the servants saw me sitting on the step pulling on my boots. He nodded, and I nodded back before setting off down the path and letting myself out through the main gate.

I couldn't see any of Shey's guards, but they usually kept out of sight. They were probably hiding in the trees, watching me now, but it didn't matter. They had been told a little of what we intended to do at the stone circle, but not enough to scare them too much. They thought it was some sort of rite to combat the dark power of the mages; when they saw me heading in that direction now, they would merely think I was setting out a little ahead of the others.

Soon I was among the trees, approaching the stones – the lair of the dragon. As I stepped over the soft ground, my feet cracked the occasional twig. A white mist lay close to the ground, but there was still enough light to avoid walking into a tree or stumbling over a log. I emerged at the foot of the hill, looking up at the standing stones, which were just visible against the cloudless sky. The brightest of the stars were out now, but the moon wouldn't be up for several hours yet.

My heart was beating fast. Would I really be able to get Alice back?

CHAPTER 18
THE TALONS OF THE MORRIGAN

I walked steadily up the hill, shivering with a chill that suddenly travelled the length of my spine. It was the usual warning that something from the dark was near, but I paid little heed, intent on my purpose.

Moments later I was standing within the circle of stones, close to the pit that we had dug for the Fiend. All I could hear was my own rapid heartbeats and breathing. The mist seemed to be thickening and rising in snake-like coils. I spun slowly on my heels, checking the area through a full three hundred and sixty degrees. The mist seemed to be rising up from the ground and there was a lot of it. It just didn't seem normal. Could it be the breath of the dragon? I wondered.

No, that was absurd. Dragons weren't fire-breathers with hot breath; they were huge elemental spirits of the air. This was just ordinary mist.

Then I saw a sudden shimmer in the air directly opposite the pit. I was face to face with Alice. My heart gave a lurch, but then I saw that she wasn't smiling; she didn't seem at all pleased to see me – she looked terrified. Her face was caked with dirt and the whites of her wild eyes were showing, her hair matted and her mouth twisted in a grimace of terror. She seemed to be standing behind that shimmering curtain. It looked so flimsy. Surely it would be easy just to step through . . .

All at once Alice thrust her left hand towards me. It came right through into the world where I stood. 'Help me, Tom!' she cried. She seemed to be shouting, but her voice was muffled and faint. 'You've got to pull me through. I can't do it alone!'

Without hesitation, I gripped her hand firmly; my left hand squeezing her left hand – which felt so cold: it was as if I was holding a dead person.

I pulled hard, but Alice seemed to resist. Was she

stuck? Was something holding her back? I tugged even harder, but then the grip on my hand tightened and it really hurt. It was as if Alice was trying to crush my finger bones. Then, as I was dragged forward against my will, Alice's face began to change. It wasn't her. It was the face of Scarabek!

I tried to resist, but the grass was slippery, my feet lost their purchase, my staff went flying from my hand – and I was dragged into the shimmering curtain, the doorway to the dark.

There was a bright flash of yellow light, and Scarabek jerked my arm and then released her grip very suddenly, sending me spinning away from her. I hit the ground hard and rolled over several times before coming to a halt against a tree trunk, which knocked the breath from my body.

I rose up onto my knees, gasping, and quickly glanced about me. I was in a wood, and all the trees looked huge. That was strange enough, but everything was also bathed in a silver light. It was as if it radiated from everything – trees, ground and sky – and I knew one thing for certain: I had left the world I knew far behind.

Suddenly I realized the truth. This wasn't the dark. I was back in the Tech Duinn, the Hollow Hills – the place where Pan had taken me in spirit.

I looked up at Scarabek. She gave me an evil smile, but she seemed to be fading. I remembered what Shey had told us. Witches could not stay here for very long.

'I'm leaving you here, boy! I'm handing you over to the Morrigan. She'll come for you at the twelfth peal of the midnight bell! You won't forget that, I'm sure! And try not to forget *who you are!*' Scarabek cried in a mocking voice.

And then she was gone, leaving me to my fate.

I got to my feet, her final words spinning around inside my head. Forgetfulness! That was a real danger. What was it that Pan had told me?

Memories bleed away into the silver light and they are lost for ever. Only heroes can endure . . .

The heroes were those of Ireland – the ancients; the great ones such as Cuchulain. Despite her magic, even a Celtic witch couldn't stay here for long. So what chance had I? I was here in the Otherworld – both in body and in soul. How could I hope to survive against the Morrigan? I had salt and iron in my pockets, and my silver chain tied about my waist. However, they couldn't hurt a goddess. I remembered my fight with the Ordeen back in Greece – how she had simply shrugged off the silver chain I had cast about her.

I'm not entirely sure what happened next – but I suddenly found myself crawling on all fours rather than walking, and I felt befuddled and disorientated. I was searching for the staff, which had been knocked out of my grasp. Where was it? I desperately needed a weapon; I knew instinctively that without one I couldn't survive.

Midnight was fast approaching, and a terrible creature would come for me then. But what was it? Some sort of daemon? All I could remember was that a witch had sent it. She wanted revenge for something I'd done to her. But what had I done? What was it?

Why couldn't I recall these things properly? My

mind was whirling with fragments of memory – pieces that I couldn't fit together. Was I already under some sort of dark enchantment? I wondered. I suddenly felt cold, very cold. Something from the dark was drawing close now.

In a panic, I leaped to my feet and desperately began to sprint through the trees, hindered by branches and thorny bushes that scratched and tore but not caring. I just *had* to get away.

I could hear something chasing me now, but it wasn't on foot. There was a furious flapping of gigantic wings. I glanced back over my shoulder and wished I hadn't, because what I saw increased my terror and panic.

I was being chased by an immense black crow.

A fragment of my shattered memory fell into place.

The huge crow was the Morrigan, the bloodthirsty Old God of the Celtic witches. She scratched her victims to mark them for death. She haunted battle-fields and pecked out the eyes of the dying.

A second fragment of memory slotted into its correct position.

This one filled me with hope. I knew that I still had a slim chance of escaping her. Ahead lay a church of some sort: once inside, I would be safe from the goddess. Could I reach it before I was seized by the Morrigan? I had dreamed this situation so many times, but now it was real. Were it not for for that recurrent nightmare, this silver-lit world of the Hollow Hills would have snatched every last bit of my memory. I wondered if this ability to learn from my dreams was another gift I'd inherited from Mam.

Churches weren't usually places of refuge from the dark. Priests might think so, but spooks certainly didn't. Nevertheless, somehow I knew that I had to reach this one – or face death.

I'd been running hard, taking little heed of obstacles such as fallen logs and roots. Inevitably I tripped and went down. I got to my knees and looked up at my pursuer.

A dreadful creature was standing before me wearing a black, bloody gown that came down to her ankles, part woman, part crow. Her feet were bare and her toenails were talons – as were her fingernails – but she had a huge feathered head with a deadly beak.

She began to shift her shape. The beak shrank, the bird-eyes changed, until the head became human in appearance.

A third fragment of memory clicked into place.

I knew that face. It was the Celtic witch, Scarabek. No doubt the Morrigan had taken on that identity to remind me of my crime against the witches who worshipped her.

All at once, in the distance, I heard the chime of a bell. Was it a church bell? If so, I could follow that sound to its source and take refuge!

It was worth a try, so on the second stroke I leaped to my feet and began to run towards the sound. I suddenly wondered how far away it was. Could I get there in time? The third peal sounded very near, but I could sense the Morrigan behind me, gliding closer and closer with every rapid step. I glanced back and saw that her face had been replaced by the huge crow's head. The sharp beak was open wide, the pointed talons lunging towards me, ready to tear my flesh, mangle my body and scatter my splintered bones.

But now, through the trees, I glimpsed the silvery outline of a building. It was little more than a chapel with a small bell-tower. If only I could reach it!

As I got nearer, however, its outline began to shimmer and slowly shift its shape. The sharp angles softened, the tower disappeared, and it settled into the form of a burial mound. There was more: beneath the dome of the grass-covered roof lay a structure of gleaming white stone. Now I could see an open doorway with an intricately carved stone lintel; absolute darkness waited within.

The Morrigan's talons raked towards my left shoulder, but I twisted away and dived through the small square entrance to that dark refuge. When I hit the ground, it felt soft; there was a covering of yellow straw, and I rolled over a couple of times before coming to a halt. I let my eyes slowly adjust to the dark – and soon I was able to make out my surroundings.

I took a couple of deep breaths, then came up into a crouch and looked about me. In the centre of the high ceiling of the mysterious chapel hung a seven-branched golden candelabrum, the thin candles blue and almost transparent. But the dim light didn't reach the four corners of the chamber, where darkness gathered in impenetrable pools.

However, most significantly, the mysterious silver light had completely disappeared. The chapel was indeed a refuge from the Otherworld, and my mind, which had become increasingly sluggish and forgetful, felt sharp and clear again, and I recalled everything that had happened.

I heard a low growl and then the padding of heavy feet. Out of the shadows emerged a monstrous hound. I began to tremble. Claw and her fully grown pups, Blood and Bone, were fearsome beasts, but this hound was the size of a Shire dray-horse, as big and powerful as all three wolfhounds put together.

Was it the guardian of this place? If so, I had little chance against such a creature. But I didn't need to defend myself, because an even bigger monster emerged from the shadows and put an enormous hand on the hound's head to restrain it.

CHAPTER 19
THE HOUND OF CALANN

He was a giant of a man with a wild mane of coarse red hair. He carried a spear in his right hand and a sword at his belt.

His striking red hair suddenly drew my attention again. Although there was no breeze, the hair seemed to be moving. It was standing on end and writhing slowly, like underwater reeds moving in a swirling current.

'You're safe here, boy,' he said in a deep booming voice as he settled down next to the magnificent hound. 'This beast won't touch you. It's what's out there that you should fear. I fear the Morrigan too, but she can't enter here. This is a *sidhe* – a place of refuge. Do you have a name?'

My throat was dry, and I had to swallow before I could speak. 'Tom Ward,' I replied.

'And what do you do, Tom? What brings you here?'

'I'm an apprentice spook. My master and I fight the dark. I was tricked by a witch into entering this Otherworld – she wants the Morrigan to hunt me down.'

'Well, as long as you stay within this sidhe she can't touch you. Not even a goddess can enter. But it wouldn't be wise to stay too long. Time passes differently here. It doesn't flow at the same rate as it does back on earth. It moves forward in great surges. It is nearing midnight. Very soon the bells will chime the hour. At the twelfth peal, time will suddenly lurch forward: in one second spent here, many long years will have passed back in your world. Everyone you know will be dead. Go quickly while you still have something to return to.'

'I want to get back, but I don't know the way. And how can I get past the Morrigan?'

'You could fight her. I've fought her before, but it

always ends in pain, and I wake up here and wait for my strength to return.'

'Who are you?' I asked.

'They once called me the Hound of Calann because I killed this dog here with my bare hands. Now, in the afterlife, we're bound together.'

I remembered the tale Shey had told us. 'So you're Cuchulain – one of the great heroes of Ireland . . .'

The giant smiled at that. 'Is that how they describe me, Tom? I like that. What else do they say about me?'

'They say that you're resting here and will return when Ireland needs you.'

Cuchulain laughed. 'Me – return? I don't think so! One life was enough for me, short as it was. I've done with killing men. No, I won't be going back, that's for sure. But I've a good mind to help *you* get back. I'm in the mood for a fight – though I must warn you, I'm not the best of men to accompany you. In battle a great fury comes upon me and a red mist clouds my vision. In that state, I've killed friends as well as enemies. I've regretted it afterwards, but that doesn't undo what's been done. It doesn't bring back the dead. So beware! But the offer is there – take it or leave it. Though don't spend too long making up your mind now.'

The huge hound lay down and closed its eyes, and a silence fell between me and Cuchulain. After a few moments his head nodded onto his chest and his eyes closed too.

If I accepted the hero's offer of help, there was no guarantee that he could really protect me against the Morrigan. Hadn't he just said that when he fought her, it ended in pain and suffering? He always lost. Then there was the battle frenzy that came over him – while fighting *her* he could just as easily kill *me*. But if I stayed here, I thought, I was as good as dead. I would never see anyone I cared about again. Although I knew now that Alice was lost to me, there was still my family. And the Spook and Grimalkin. Even my chance to bind the Fiend would be gone, and I'd be a stranger in an unknown world. I had a duty to fight the dark. I needed to complete my training and become a spook in my own right. No, I had to leave the sidhe – and as soon as possible, whatever the risk.

'You know a way back to my world?' I said to Cuchulain.

The dog growled in its sleep and he patted its head, his own eyes still closed. 'I know several doors that lead back: the nearest lies not far from here. We could be halfway there before the goddess even realizes we've left this refuge.'

'I *have* to escape,' I told him. 'Will you help me?'

Cuchulain opened one eye and gave me a lopsided grin. 'My heart quickens!' he cried. 'I can smell the blood of the Morrigan. It's worth a go. This time I could win. This time I could strike off her head!' He laughed. 'You see, I'm an eternal optimist. Never give up! That's the true quality that marks out a hero. Never give up, even when things look hopeless! And I think you have that quality, boy. You too are a hero!'

'I don't think so,' I said, shaking my head. 'I'm just a spook's apprentice – I often get scared when facing the dark.'

Cuchulain smiled. 'Even heroes are sometimes

afraid, Tom. It takes the bravery of a hero to admit fear. Besides, you are here in the sidhe, and still breathing. Were you made of less, you would have been destroyed the moment you entered this place.'

He got to his feet and picked up his huge spear. 'Have you no weapons, Tom?' he demanded.

'I use a spook's staff, but I lost it when I was dragged through the doorway from my world. I have nothing but salt and iron and my silver chain . . .'

'The Morrigan won't be bothered much by salt and iron, and the chain would only bind her for moments. She'd shift her shape and slip out of it in the twinkling of an eye. Here – take this dagger,' he said, reaching into his leather jerkin and handing me a weapon. 'Strike her hard with this. She'll feel it, mark my words!'

To Cuchulain it might have been a dagger, but he was a huge man, over twice the size of the village smith at Chipenden. The blade he handed me was a sword. It looked a very special sword too, no doubt crafted for a king. The hilt was ornate – shaped like the head of some sort of beast. With a shock, I recognized it. It was a skelt, the creature that hid in crevices near water, then scuttled out to drink the blood of its victims. The skelt's long snout formed the serrated blade of the sword; its eyes were two large rubies. It made sense – Ireland had lots of bogs and water, which would be home to skelts, so the sword had been fashioned in its likeness.

I took the handle in my left hand and tested it for balance. It felt right – almost as if it had been made for me.

Then I saw that the blade itself was crafted from a silver alloy. Such a weapon could destroy a daemon. Although it was not effective against one of the Old Gods, the blade could still injure the Morrigan and buy precious time while I made my escape.

Suddenly I saw that blood was dripping from the sword and forming a small red pool on the ground. For a moment I thought that I'd cut myself on the sharp blade; but then, to my astonishment, I realized that the blood was weeping from the two red ruby eyes.

Cuchulain grinned. 'It likes you, boy!' he exclaimed.

'It likes you a lot! The first time I held that blade it dripped a little blood. But nothing like as much as that! You *belong* to the blade. It *owns* you. You'll belong to it until the day you die.'

How could a sword *own* me? I wondered. Surely it was I who owned the *sword*? However, this wasn't the time to contradict Cuchulain.

'Are you ready, Tom?' he asked.

I nodded.

'We have to move fast. As soon as we're clear of the sidhe, turn sharp left. About fifty paces will bring us to a ford. It's not an easy crossing, but on the other side lies a cave. Run straight in and don't slow down. The far wall is the doorway back to the world of humans – but to pass through you must run at it at full pelt. Do you hear?'

I nodded again. 'I'm ready,' I told him.

Cuchulain gripped his spear and sprinted out of the sidhe, the huge hound at his side. I ran after him, holding my sword ready. Once more we were bathed in that sickly silver light. I forced myself to concentrate, fearing for my memory.

Once outside, there was no sign of the Morrigan. Cuchulain and his hound were pulling away, and I struggled to keep up, but then I caught sight of the river ahead, a fat silver snake meandering through the trees. Suddenly I found myself alongside Cuchulain. Had I somehow managed to speed up or had he slowed down?

I glanced to my right and saw that he was now staggering. When we'd left the sidhe, his left shoulder and arm had been strong and muscular. Now they were withered, so feeble that he could barely grasp his spear. As I watched, he transferred it to his right hand and stumbled onwards, slowing with every stride, as if about to fall. I remembered Shey's story: during Cuchulain's life he'd been weakened by a witch's curse. Was the Morrigan now exerting her power over him, renewing the spell?

I heard a new sound then – the harsh chatter of crows. The branches of the trees ahead of us were bowed down under their weight. Was the Morrigan amongst them? I wondered. The answer came quickly.

No! A monstrous crow as big as Cuchulain was flying directly towards us, claws extended, beak agape. As the Morrigan swooped through the trees, I swerved away to the left, but Cuchulain hefted his spear and stabbed at her. Feathers flew and the goddess screamed. He'd hurt her, and she landed heavily. But then she flew at him again, talons lashing out.

I turned, ready to go to his aid, gripping the sword tightly. They were grappling in close combat, her talons tearing at his flesh, but I also saw blood-spattered feathers on the ground. Both of them were bleeding. The Morrigan was shrieking like a banshee witch, while Cuchulain roared and bellowed like a beast.

I moved closer, waiting for my chance to stab her with the sword. I saw that the hound was watching too. Why didn't it go and help its master? I looked closely at Cuchulain and realized that he was starting to change. The battle fury was coming upon him. One eye seemed to be bulging out of his forehead and his hair was standing up and thickening like the sharp quills of a hedgehog. The skin of his face was rippling, his teeth bared in a snarl, as though he wanted to bite off the crow head that confronted him.

I ran forward, raising my sword to strike the goddess. Luckily I never got close enough to do so – it would have been the end of me. Mad with rage, Cuchulain reached out with his left hand and seized the neck of the hound. In spite of his withered arm, insane anger lent him strength. He swung the hound against the trunk of the nearest tree. The massive trunk shuddered with the impact, but the head of the hound broke open like an egg, splattering brains and red gore on wood and ground.

Cuchulain threw the lifeless body away and then glared about him. For a moment his eyes rested upon me and terror froze me to the spot. Then his gaze moved on, but rather than going for the Morrigan with renewed fury, he attacked a mighty oak tree! He swung his spear at it again and again, the blows resounding through the forest. Branches broke and fell to the silver grass in splinters. Then he began to drive the point of his spear into the trunk. Deeper and deeper went the blade with each blow, shards of wood flying up into the air. But my eyes were no longer on Cuchulain. I was staring at the giant crow, which was changing even as I watched.

Once more the Morrigan took the shape of Scarabek. She smiled and came towards me. Distracted by his own rage, Cuchulain was no longer a threat to her. Now she was coming for *me*!

I turned and sprinted towards the river, as he'd instructed. When I reached its bank, I saw to my dismay that the water was high and fast-flowing, a silver torrent that I could not cross. Where was the ford? The Morrigan was strolling towards me now, almost casually, as if she had all the time in the world . . .

All the time in the world? That was exactly what I *didn't* have. Midnight was approaching, and as soon as the bell had pealed twelve times, years would have passed back home. I scanned the riverbank and spotted the stepping stones. They lay to my left – eight of them, their tops just visible above the water.

The Morrigan saw where I was heading and began to run, but I reached the ford first and took a mighty leap towards the first stone. It was wet and slippery, and I almost lost my balance. But I managed to jump across to the second, and then the third. When I reached the fifth, I looked back. The Morrigan was leaping from stone to stone too. I'd half hoped that she wouldn't be able to cross running water. But, although in the guise of a witch, she was a goddess, and the torrent proved no barrier to her. There was just one more stone, then I could jump up onto the river-bank. However, the Morrigan was close behind me now. I would never make it. So I turned and held up my sword, preparing to defend myself.

She came for me, her hands outstretched, her talons glinting. I swung the sword with all my strength. It struck her hard on the right shoulder. Blood spurted up, and she screamed and fell into the water with a tremendous splash. This was my chance. I made it to the final slippery stone, then leaped up onto the bank, my heart pounding.

I could see the entrance to the cave ahead, a dark gaping mouth in the silver cliff. I hurried towards it. At one point I looked back. The Morrigan had risen and was following me again. She wasn't even running. Did she think that I'd be unable to escape?

The cave was gloomy, but not as dark as it had first seemed; it was gleaming with that same mysterious silver light that illuminated all of the Otherworld but the sidhe. I studied the back wall. It looked hard – and solid. I ran towards it as Cuchulain had instructed, but at the last moment I slowed a little and flinched, anticipating the impact.

I collided with solid rock – a tremendous blow jarred me from head to toe. I stumbled backwards, the sword spinning from my hand, and lay there, stunned. My head and knees hurt. I could taste blood in my mouth.

What had gone wrong? Perhaps the Morrigan had worked some type of enchantment, I thought. Was that why she'd strolled after me, not even bothering to run? I came up onto my knees and crawled across to the sword. I took it in my left hand, and managed to get to my feet before taking slow painful steps towards the mouth of the cave. When I reached it, the goddess was only a dozen paces away, advancing steadily.

I took a deep breath to calm my fears and readied the sword in my hand. But the nearer she came, the more my confidence ebbed away. I saw that her gown was unmarked – there was no sign of the wound I'd inflicted. A goddess of such power would heal quickly. The silver blade could certainly hurt her and slow her down – but not destroy her. All I could do was buy a little time for myself . . .

Time! No sooner had the thought entered my head than the first peal of the midnight bell rang out in the distance. I knew that when the twelfth one sounded, time back on earth would lurch forward. I was desperately wondering what to do next, and thought of what Cuchulain had said about the doorway.

The second chime rang out . . .

Full pelt – you had to run hard and fast at that back wall of the cave. Just now, I'd slowed and flinched at the last moment. It was difficult to imagine an impact harder than the one I'd suffered, but it had to be done. It was my only chance of getting back to the world I knew. But first I had to deal with the Morrigan . . .

She ran at me now, claws outstretched, eyes blazing with a ferocious anger. As she lunged towards me, the bell tolled for the third time. I spun away to the left, and she missed me, her talons gouging the rock close to my head.

Then I struck out at her with my sword, but the blow was delivered clumsily and in haste. The blade clanged against solid rock, jarring my arm. The bell pealed again . . .

The next few seconds passed in a blur, and I knew that I had to bring our struggle to a swift end. Above the sounds of my laboured breathing, the snarls of the Morrigan and the scuffling of my boots against the rocky ground, I could hear the slow, steady peals of the bell. By now I'd lost count. How long before the twelfth chime?

I thought back to the cave wall: I had to *believe* I could pass through it. I began to focus my mind. Strangely, as

I did so, I felt the sword vibrate in my hand, and a single drop of blood fell from the left ruby eye.

As the goddess ran at me again, I feinted to the left, then changed to a right cut, bringing my sword down fast, almost horizontally, towards her. It was a perfect blow. As if it was slicing through butter, the sword took her head clean from her shoulders. It fell to the ground with a sickening crunch, but then went spinning and rolling away down the hill towards the silver river below.

For a moment the Morrigan's headless body stood there swaying, the neck spurting blood. Then, rather than falling, she staggered off down the slope in pursuit of her head. It seemed unlikely that she'd catch it before it rolled into the river.

Wasting no time, I hurried back into the cave. Faster and faster I ran, straight towards the waiting wall of solid rock. It took all my willpower not to slow down, not to flinch or twist away. I still felt a tremendous blow – and then everything went black.

I heard a distant final peal of the bell. Then silence.

CHAPTER
20
NOBODY WILL HEAR YOU SCREAM

Even before I opened my eyes I felt a cool breeze on my face and the grass beneath my prone body.

I sat up and looked about me; I realized I was still holding the bloody sword. It was almost dark now. I was at the centre of the circle of standing stones at Kenmare. But had I returned in time? How long had passed – a century?

I got to my feet and headed towards the pit. It was hard to tell in the poor light, but it looked the same. Had it been abandoned, I thought, even a few months would have filled it with grass and weeds.

Then I saw my staff lying on the ground. That gave me a flash of real hope. The Spook would have come in search of me. He would have found the staff and taken it away – not left it lying there.

So I picked up my staff and set off for Shey's house. When I arrived at the gate, there were two guards prowling about, but they nodded me through as though nothing had happened.

When I walked into the hallway, the Spook and Grimalkin were standing there. The witch assassin was carrying the stakes, wrapped in sacking, the Spook holding his staff. I felt so relieved. Clearly less time had passed here than in the Otherworld. They both looked at me in astonishment.

'Are you hurt, lad?' my master asked.

I shook my head. 'A few cuts and bruises but nothing serious.'

'What happened? Where have you been?' he demanded.

'That sword!' exclaimed Grimalkin, her eyes wide with astonishment, before I could answer. 'Let me see it!'

She put down her bundle of spears and I handed it to

her. The witch assassin examined it closely but avoided touching the silver-alloy blade.

She looked at me. 'Do you know what this is?' she cried, peering at the strange marks engraved on the hilt and touching the carving of the skelt's head.

I shook my head. What did she mean?

'It's a "hero sword" crafted by one of the Old Gods called Hephaestus,' she told me. 'Only three were ever made, and this is the best of them!'

I smiled at her. 'I met the hero!' I confirmed. 'We were in the Otherworld and he gave me his sword. Without it I wouldn't be here. The Morrigan attacked me and I cut off her head.'

'The Morrigan will heal herself,' said Grimalkin. 'You can count on that. But I'm thinking of our forthcoming struggle against the Fiend. This weapon gives us a far better chance of success. It goes by another name that is peculiar to it alone – perhaps a name that better defines its purpose. It has been called the "Destiny Blade". The one who wields it fulfils what he was born to achieve.'

'I don't hold with that,' interrupted the Spook. 'We shape the future with each act we perform. There is no such thing as destiny. It's just an illusion – something we think we can see retrospectively.'

'I disagree,' said Grimalkin.

'Aye, I thought you might, so let's agree to differ,' my master told her. 'The lad's hurt and weary. We all need to be at our best to bind the Fiend. We'll leave it until tomorrow.'

Grimalkin nodded in agreement.

'So get yourself to bed, lad,' said the Spook, looking at me sternly. 'You can tell us the full story in the morning.'

I woke up, aware that someone – or something – was in my room. I could see the silhouette of a tall form against the grey dawn light shining through the curtains. I sat up quickly and realized that it was Grimalkin.

'Stand up, boy!' she ordered. 'We have much to do today.'

I had fallen asleep on top of the covers, still wearing my shirt and breeches. I got to my feet as she'd commanded. The witch moved closer; she towered over me, a full head taller than I was.

'Take off your shirt.'

When I hesitated, Grimalkin shook her head and smiled, her black-painted lips parting enough for me to glimpse the sharp teeth behind. 'I've seen skinny ribs before!' she mocked. Then I saw that she was holding a grey garment in her left hand.

I unbuttoned my shirt and peeled it off. Grimalkin began expertly draping the garment around my chest. As she did so, she paused, noting the mark on my arm where Alice had once dug her nails into my flesh. 'This is Alice's mark, isn't it?' she asked me. I nodded, my heart heavy at the thought that I was never going to see my friend again.

I turned my attention to the garment that Grimalkin was fitting. It was some sort of shirt but seemed to be padded at the shoulders. There was another padded section that ran diagonally from my right shoulder down towards my left hip. The witch buttoned the shirt quickly with nimble fingers, and then, from a scabbard on one of the leather straps that crisscrossed her own body, she withdrew a pair of scissors.

I flinched and stepped backwards. These were the scissors she used to snip away the thumb-bones of her enemies. Some said that she did so while they still breathed.

But it wasn't my bones that she wanted. Quickly she cut away some material, trimming the bottom of the shirt and then the sleeves, so that they now finished above the elbow.

'This is a padded undershirt,' she explained. 'You'll wear it to stop the straps and scabbard chafing against your skin.'

She now held a length of leather in her hand; attached to it was a scabbard similar to the ones that she wore. She set to work fitting it. After first trimming its length with her scissors, using a needle and thread she tacked it to the undershirt with just a couple of deft stitches.

Once she'd finished, Grimalkin picked up the sword and handed it to me. 'Sheath it!' she commanded.

'Am I to use it right-handed?' I asked.

'You'll use either hand, but since your primary weapon is your staff, which you wield with your left hand, you should draw the sword with the other.'

I sheathed the sword.

'Now draw it as quickly as you can!'

I obeyed.

'Sheath and draw it again . . .'

When I'd done as she asked, Grimalkin repositioned the leather strap, and this time used several stitches to attach it firmly to the undershirt.

'Now,' she said with a grim smile, 'it's time to go down to the cellar . . .'

The cellar was situated far below the living quarters of the house. I obediently followed Grimalkin down the long spiral of stone steps. Inside, the flagged floor was empty save for a table pushed back against the near wall. About a dozen torches in wall brackets lit the area. It looked like it had recently been swept.

Grimalkin closed the heavy wooden door behind us, and then turned the key in the lock before removing it and tossing it onto the table.

'Why have we come down here?' I asked, my mouth suddenly dry.

'For one thing we have plenty of space,' she replied. 'But not only that – down in this cellar, nobody will hear you scream.'

I took a step backwards. Grimalkin took one towards me. 'There's nowhere to run, Thomas Ward,' she said, her voice quiet and filled with malice. 'You impaled me once with your staff. I owe you for that – and I always pay my debts. Nothing less than your life will suffice, so draw the sword and defend yourself – if you can!'

It was true that I had once driven my staff through her shoulder, pinning her to a tree. Then, I had been acting in self-defence – she had been hunting me down, ready to take my life. But since then we had fought together side by side; I'd thought that we were now allies, and that Grimalkin had come to Kenmare in order to help us bind the Fiend. Had it all been a lie? I wondered. Was her need for vengeance so great? Had she rescued me from the fort just so that she could put an end to me in this cellar herself?

I was scared and my knees trembled. I barely managed to get the sword clear of its scabbard before she attacked. Drawing two blades at once, Grimalkin ran directly towards me. I raised the Destiny Blade and managed to deflect the one in her left hand, twisting away so that the other blade missed my left ear by less than an inch.

Before I'd recovered my balance properly, she whirled towards me again. In a panic, I chopped down at her head, but she parried and smiled grimly before stabbing towards my left shoulder. I wasn't fast enough, and I felt a sharp pain as the blade cut into my flesh. How badly was I hurt? I glanced at the wound and saw blood dribbling down towards my elbow.

To check the severity of my wound was a foolish mistake – one that almost cost me my life. The moment I glanced down, Grimalkin took advantage of my lapse and launched an all-out attack. I stumbled under her onslaught, but somehow her blades missed me.

I rolled away and jumped to my feet. She approached me again, her eyes glittering, her mouth open wide, as if she was going to take a bite out of my flesh. Those teeth, which she had filed to deadly points, were one of the scariest things about the witch assassin.

I was beginning to despair now. What chance did I have against Grimalkin? How could I hope to beat the most deadly assassin the Malkin clan had ever produced? I realized that I had just one faint hope. Somehow, in the heat of battle, I had to concentrate my mind and try to slow down time itself. That gift, inherited from Mam, had saved my life on more than one occasion. I had to attempt it now.

Before I could carry out my plan, Grimalkin charged. A sudden anger surged through me. What was she doing? I didn't deserve to die in this cellar. And if she killed me now, the Fiend would be waiting to torment my soul. With a surge of new-found confidence, I stepped forward and swung my sword at her with all my strength, forcing her to lean back quickly, then step to the side. I attacked again, and this time switched the sword from my right to my left hand. It was a trick taught to me by the Spook when we practised with our staffs. That's how I had wounded her last time.

It almost caught her out again, but she dodged away to safety and then came forward once more. I took a deep breath and started to focus, drawing on the power that lay deep within me.

Concentrate! Squeeze time. Slow it. Make it halt!

Grimalkin was moving towards me, her approach almost taking the form of a dance. She was balancing on her toes and flexing her knees, skipping away to the left, raising her arm to deliver a fatal blow to my heart. But her movements were slowing, and I was faster. My blade intercepted hers and dashed it from her hand.

Gleaming in the torchlight, the assassin's dagger spun over and over again, slow as a feather, falling gently towards the flags. But then it halted. It was immobile, frozen in space, hovering above the floor. I had actually halted time!

I reversed the movement of my blade, slashing it back towards the witch's neck. Grimalkin was helpless; I had won.

I watched my sword slice towards her unprotected throat. But then I noticed something else. Grimalkin was frozen in time, helpless, but she was also looking me in the eye – and smiling! She was smiling at me while my blade was inches from her throat!

At the last moment I pulled the blade upwards so that it missed her. Then I stepped away and went into a crouch. Why hadn't I killed her while I had the chance? What was wrong with me? On the island of Mona I'd been unable to kill Bony Lizzie when I'd had the opportunity. I had held back then because she was Alice's mother. But what was happening here? I asked myself.

And suddenly I knew. I relaxed and allowed time to move on once more. Grimalkin quickly sheathed her other blade and moved towards me. She was still smiling.

I realized then that it had been some sort of trial. She'd been testing me. Then she spoke.

'I once consulted Martha Ribstalk, then the foremost scryer in Pendle,' Grimalkin said, 'and she told me that a child had just been born who represented a force that might somehow counter that of the Fiend. Powerful though Martha was, someone was hiding him from her sight. I now believe that this protector was your mother; you are that child – and my ally in this struggle against my sworn enemy. Together we will succeed. It is meant to be. It is our destiny to destroy the Fiend.'

My hands started to shake a little. Now that it was over I felt a rush of relief.

'I wanted to strike fear into you. I needed to put you under pressure so that you would fight as if for your life. I have now had the opportunity to study your use of the sword, and know what needs to be done to improve it. I've spoken with John Gregory and told him that I need at least a week to train you. He has agreed. Once you reach the required standard, we will attempt to bind the Fiend. It's our best hope.'

'I'm going to fight the Fiend with this sword?'

Grimalkin smiled again. 'Not exactly – but what I teach you will be vital, because denizens of the dark, the Fiend's servants, will seek you out. They will try to hunt you down, so you will need skill to wield that sword. It could mean the difference between life and death. As I told you, the sword has another name – the Destiny Blade – and despite what your master says, each of its keepers fulfils his destiny – that which he was meant to achieve in this life – while he bears it.'

'That sounds too much like fate,' I said; 'the idea that the future is fixed. I'm with the Spook on that. I believe that each of us has some free will, some freedom of choice.'

'Child, maybe that is true, but I do believe you have a destiny – you were born to destroy the Fiend. And you are the hunter of the dark. Now that you have that blade, it will truly begin to fear you! Do you remember how you sliced off the head of the Morrigan?'

Suddenly I knew what Grimalkin expected of me. 'You want me to do that to the Fiend?'

'We impale and then behead. I will then bury the head elsewhere. It will give you time to work out a permanent solution so that he can be destroyed for all time.'

'I almost killed you just then,' I told her. 'The test went too far . . .'

Grimalkin shook her head. 'I know when I will die. Martha Ribstalk told me that too. I am not meant to die here at your hands.'

I nodded. I knew the Spook would have thought Grimalkin's faith in that prophecy foolish indeed.

CHAPTER
~21~
FROZEN IN TIME

Bill Arkwright had once spent six months training me, with an emphasis on the physical aspects of the spook's trade, particularly combat – fighting with staffs. He had been a hard taskmaster, at times verging on cruelty, and I had ended up covered in bruises. It had been a painful and exhausting experience.

That, however, was nothing compared to what I went through in the week I spent under Grimalkin's tutelage. Much of my suffering was caused by the sheer terror I felt, fighting head to head with the witch assassin. Her appearance was daunting enough, but in addition, her eyes blazed with an intimidating ferocity, and I never knew which blade she would draw from the many sheaths around her body.

She also possessed a physical strength that I could not hope to match yet. I had to keep out of range. Once she got a hand on me I invariably ended up on my back, with the breath driven from my body and a blade at my throat.

She cut me too, more than once – it would have been good to have Alice at hand with her healing herbs and poultices. The pain of losing my best friend was still undiminished – the sharp edges of Grimalkin's blades were nothing compared to that.

I soon became skilled with the sword – which now felt like an extension of myself – but the witch assassin was quick to tell me that this was barely the beginning of what I would need to know. She said that I would improve each time I fought for my life against an opponent who wanted to kill me – always assuming that I survived the encounter.

One of the skills I was made to practise over and over again was stopping time while in combat. As the week progressed, my control steadily improved. As I'd already shown, by using it I could match an opponent as deadly as Grimalkin.

All too soon that week of intense training came to a close, and we were ready to face our greatest challenge yet.

As the sun set, we left Shey's house and approached the pit. There were just the three of us: the Spook, Grimalkin and me. I was wearing my cloak, but beneath it lay the Destiny Blade in its scabbard. The blood jar lay in the pocket of my breeches. During my training with the witch, the Spook had been adding to his Bestiary, updating it where possible and writing a new section on our preparations for binding the Fiend.

In my years with the Spook, I had always expected Alice to take part in this task – but it was not to be. She was gone for ever now, and I had to learn to accept it.

The rigger and his mate were waiting beside the huge wooden frame they had erected above the pit. They both looked scared, but so far they had done a good job: suspended from the block and tackle, hanging horizontally, was the huge flat stone that would seal the pit. To one side lay the heavy rock that would finally be placed on top. It had a ring embedded in it make lifting it easier.

Heaped close to the pit was the mound of soil that I had worked so hard to excavate. Mixed into it was a large amount of salt and iron. They were not likely to have much power against the Fiend, but the Spook thought that if it weakened him even slightly, it was worth a try. If we succeeded in binding him, that mixture would fill the pit.

If we failed . . . the Fiend would be quick to take his revenge for what I had done; he'd first deal with me, then kill the Spook and Grimalkin. After that our souls would face an eternity of torment.

I noticed that Grimalkin was carrying two sacks: one contained the spears and nails; the other was made of leather and appeared to be empty. It looked quite new – had she stitched it herself? I wondered. She placed both sacks on the ground and, already wearing her leather gloves, carefully unwrapped the four long spears. Beside them were a number of long broad-headed silver- alloy nails, and two short-handled lump-hammers for driving them into the Fiend's flesh. One of these she handed to the Spook.

It had already been agreed that the Spook and I would take up positions in the pit, ready to attack the Fiend from below, while, from above, Grimalkin would attempt to drive her spear through his heart. Then, if we succeeded thus far, we would nail him to the rock.

By now the sun had gone down and the light was beginning to fail, but the pit was lit by seven lanterns; three were suspended from the wooden gantry, the others placed on the ground close to its four corners.

The Spook climbed down into the pit and I followed. Despite the solid rock base that had halted my excavations, it was very deep, the Spook's head barely level with its rim. The witch assassin handed each of us a spear. They were slender and flexible, and had sharp points. The Spook and I took up positions at opposite corners of the pit. Above, Grimalkin held the third spear with both hands – the fourth lay on the ground beside her – and gazed down intently.

The Spook cleared his throat. 'This is the moment we've all been waiting for,' he said solemnly. 'One or more of us may lose our lives. It will be well worth it if the Fiend is successfully bound. We share the same purpose, and I thank you both for standing by my side!'

It was an astonishing declaration by my master. He had actually thanked a witch for working with him! Grimalkin gave the faintest of smiles and nodded towards him in acknowledgement.

'It's time,' said the Spook, turning his gaze towards me. 'Give me the blood jar!'

My mouth was dry and my hands shook, but I was determined to do what was necessary. I focused on controlling my breathing and calming myself. Nervously I took the jar out of my pocket, walked across the pit and handed it to him. How strange it was to think that Alice I had spent so much time worrying that the cracked jar might lose its power and enable the

Fiend to snatch us away; and now the Spook was about to destroy it.

I quickly returned to my place. For a moment the Spook stared at the small earthen jar with an expression of distaste, then held it high.

'The crack in the jar has enabled the Fiend to come close to you many times,' he said. 'I suspect he is always nearby, waiting to come and take his revenge. So I expect him to appear the very moment the jar is broken. Be ready!'

With a sudden convulsive movement the Spook hurled it up out of the pit and against one of the stout wooden props that supported the gantry. With a sharp crack, it shattered, and my knees nearly gave way.

It was done. The Fiend would arrive within seconds. Alice had always believed that if the jar broke, his response would be immediate.

However, the seconds became minutes . . . and nothing happened. I became uneasy. Maybe it would be days before he arrived. If that were the case, it would be difficult to remain vigilant. This was not what we'd expected.

And then that I felt a strong tremor under my feet. The ground was shifting. Suddenly the lanterns flickered ominously and their light began to wane. They died right down to a faint glimmer, and one of riggers gave a loud cry of fear. Directly overhead, there was a sound like a peal of thunder, and we were momentarily plunged into total darkness.

The Fiend was approaching . . .

I began to concentrate, summoning my strength. Stop time too early, and the Fiend would be unable to enter the pit; do it too late, and he would seize control – and I would be *his* prisoner, stuck like a fly trapped in amber while he did his worst.

The lanterns shone brightly once more, and with a terrifying bellow that seemed to make the whole world shake, the Fiend appeared in the pit between me and the Spook. He radiated a lurid red light of his own. Despite my terror I was filled with hope. He had come. It *could* be done.

Concentrate! Squeeze time! Make it stop!

The Fiend was three times the size of the Spook, with a broad chest, a long tail, cloven feet and the curved horns of a ram, and was covered in thick black hair. His pupils were two vertical slits, and he gave off a strong animal stench that made my stomach heave. But amidst the terror I felt, I noted with relief that the pit would be big enough after all.

The Fiend wasn't moving – controlling time had become almost second nature to me now – but neither were the Spook or Grimalkin. All was immobile and silent. My heart was still beating. I was still breathing. I had stopped time. Now I had to impale him . . .

I moved to stab towards him, but my spear moved very slowly. Even worse, my heart seemed to be slowing, each laboured beat taking longer to arrive than its predecessor. The Fiend was fighting back; trying to freeze *me* in time and release himself.

Had I left it too late? How could I hope to match his strength with my own? I asked myself. But I had to try. I couldn't give up now.

Gritting my teeth, I drove my silver spear up towards his belly – but I saw that it was moving ever more slowly. If I failed in this, the Fiend would end our lives. It would be the end of everything we had tried to do. I thrust the weapon towards him just as hard as I could, bringing all my concentration to bear. But it was as if I was frozen now.

Grimalkin . . . I thought. Couldn't she just wish him away?

That hope was snuffed out instantly. How could she? She would be just like me, trapped in an instant of time, desperately wondering what could be done. She would not wish the Fiend away because then he would escape her spears. Grimalkin had faith in me: she trusted me to defeat the Devil. *But what if I couldn't?*

And then my sight began to dim.

CHAPTER 22
THE DESTINY BLADE

Even as my vision clouded, I continued the fight, once again summoning all my concentration. Though I was facing defeat, I couldn't give up. Not now. I remembered the advice given to me by Cuchulain: I must struggle on, no matter how hopeless it seemed. And the thought of what the Fiend had been doing to Alice spurred me on to make one final effort. Even if I couldn't get her back, I could hurt him, make him pay. Even if I was losing, I would fight to the bitter end.

But then, just when it seemed that all hope was gone, there was a sudden change. I felt something yield very slightly. My heart began to thud inside my chest –

slowly at first, then faster and faster! I was in control again, my blood surging through my veins. The Fiend was standing before me, large and terrifying – but immobile. Now he was still and *I* was moving!

I thrust the silver spear up into his side. There was momentary resistance, then a spurt of black blood. I pushed it upwards even harder, deep into his hairy hide. The Fiend screamed, a noise that stabbed into my eardrums; a cry of pain and anger with the power to split the earth asunder and make the very stones bleed. It buffeted me so hard that I lost my concentration – and my grip on time.

Suddenly the Fiend burst free of my control, twisted towards me and brought his huge fist scything downwards. I ducked; felt it brush past my hair.

But time was moving freely again, and now the others were able to attack. The Fiend bellowed for a second time as the Spook plunged his own spear deep into his hairy belly, bringing him to his knees.

Above, there was a flash of forked lightning, followed immediately by a deep rumble of thunder. A storm burst overhead, torrential rain drumming into the ground. It seemed to have come from nowhere.

I looked up and saw Grimalkin balanced on the balls of her feet, taking careful aim. The witch assassin never missed – surely she wouldn't this time? My heart was in my mouth, but I needn't have feared. She thrust downwards powerfully, and her spear pierced the Fiend's back. It went right through his body and, with an explosion of black gore, the bloodied point emerged from his chest. She'd speared his heart with silver. But would it be enough?

Lightning flashed again, dividing the sky, and a fury of rain plummeted into the pit as the witch assassin threw her second spear to pierce the Fiend's body within an inch of the first. His heart was now transfixed by two silver spears. He gave a great groan of pain and bowed forward, blood and saliva dripping from his open mouth. Grimalkin now leaped down into the pit to his left. In one hand was a hammer; in the other gloved hand a fistful of silver nails. Meanwhile the Spook moved towards the Fiend's right arm.

By now the Fiend was on all fours, tossing his head like a wounded bull and roaring with pain. The witch assassin seized her chance and stabbed a nail into his left hand, then struck the broad head three times with the hammer, driving it right through his flesh to pin that huge hairy paw tightly to the rock. He twisted his head, opened his mouth wide and lunged towards her as if to bite her head from her body. But, lithe as a cat, she avoided that deadly mouth and swung the hammer back hard into his face, smashing his front teeth into fragments and leaving only broken bloody stumps.

I watched my master quickly drive a nail into the Fiend's right hand, the muscles bunching in his shoulder as he swung the heavy hammer with a rhythm and power that belied his age. Seconds later, working as a team, the Spook and Grimalkin had driven a nail through each of the Fiend's ankles. As he roared with pain, Grimalkin pointed towards me.

'His head!' she cried. 'Now! Strike off his head! Do it now!'

I drew the hero sword and stepped towards the Fiend;

as I did so, blood started to drip from both its ruby eyes. I lifted it up high, took a deep breath, tensed my muscles and brought it down towards his neck. Black blood spurted up as the blade cut into his flesh. But my arm jarred as it struck bone and sinew. The Fiend screamed, the blade jammed, and it took a couple of seconds for me to tug it free.

'Strike again!' shouted Grimalkin. 'Do it!'

Once more I brought the sword down on the same place on the neck. This time the resistance was slight, and the sword severed the Fiend's huge head from his shoulders. It fell into the pit and rolled away, to end up at Grimalkin's feet.

My eyes met the Spook's, but there was no victory there. He simply nodded.

Grimalkin seized the head by the curved horns and held it aloft. Black blood dripped from it, and the Fiend's swollen lips moved over his shattered teeth as if he was trying to speak. But his eyes had rolled up into his head; only the whites were showing. Grimalkin sprang out of the pit and pushed the head into her new leather sack. After tying the neck securely, she returned to the pit, where the Fiend's decapitated body still shuddered and writhed.

The Spook and I got our spades and quickly started to fill in the pit with the mound of iron- and salt-laced soil. I glanced up at the gantry. The rigger and his mate were nowhere to be seen. They had fled.

With torrential rain still falling, the three of us chucked soil into the pit just as fast as we could. Drenched to the skin, we worked rapidly, frantic to hide the monstrous beast, not knowing yet what he was capable of. I wondered whether, even without a head, he could tear himself free. Gradually his struggles lessened; the groans from the head in the sack were quieter too.

Some time later, the rigger and his mate returned. By then the decapitated body of the Fiend was almost covered, though the soil still twitched and heaved. Shamefaced, the two men mumbled their apologies. The Spook simply patted them on the back. With the extra hands, our progress was faster – though it took almost another hour before we had finally filled in the pit and stamped down the earth. The work completed, we stood there, looking down, our chests still heaving with the exertion. At last it was time to lower the flat stone lid onto the pit.

By now the rain had ceased, but it was slippery underfoot so we had to take care. With the rigger working the chain, Grimalkin and I grasped one side of the stone while the Spook and the rigger's mate held the other. It came down smoothly, and at the last moment we pulled our hands clear and the lid fell into position, a perfect fit.

Next the rigger's mate dragged the chain across and set the hook into the ring in the boulder. Soon it was being lifted into the air and lowered into position in the centre of the stone lid. Then, its work done, the rigger unscrewed the iron ring. Finally we heaped the last of the soil over the lid and around the boulder. Once the grass grew, it would look just like a central thirteenth standing stone amid the twelve that surrounded it. Folk would never know that the body of the Fiend lay buried here within the stone circle at Kenmare.

But Grimalkin wasn't finished yet. She added to the dragon's threat by casting a cloaking spell of her own to hide the Fiend's presence from the servants of the dark. The Spook turned his back as she completed the ritual, walking three times around the outside of the stones; as she walked, she chanted her powerful spell.

At last she came to stand beside us. It seemed that we'd succeeded. The great beast was bound; despite all his efforts, he had been unable to tear himself free. We remained standing there for some time, saying nothing, hardly able to believe what we'd just accomplished.

'The Fiend isn't bound for ever, though, is he?' I dared ask, my voice hardly more than a whisper. 'One way or another, some day he'll be free . . .'

'Nothing lasts for ever, lad,' said the Spook, frowning. 'But now he can't leave that shape because his flesh is pierced with silver and he's bound to the rock. And separating him from his head makes the binding even stronger. He'll be here until we find a way to put an end to him for good. But what I fear most is that someone or something else might release him. That's the biggest danger now.'

'That won't happen,' said Grimalkin. 'As you say, so long as the head and the body are separated, the Fiend will remain bound. At first I intended to bury the head in a different place – maybe far across the sea. But now I've thought of a better way.

'The head belongs to me now. I will be its custodian. I plan to travel back to the County and keep it near me at all times. Denizens of the dark will hunt me down. They will come after me to retrieve the head and return it here, but I will kill them one by one. I will keep it as long as I can' – Grimalkin looked down – 'though it's true that I cannot run and fight for ever. There will be too many, and they will catch me in the end.' She looked at me directly. 'While I hold them off, use the time to find a way to finish him once and for all.'

I drew the sword and held it towards her, hilt first. 'Take the sword,' I said. 'It will help!'

Grimalkin shook her head. 'No, I have my own weapons, and your need will be greater. Remember, the servants of the Fiend will follow you too. They will know what has been done – and recognize your part in it. Besides, you are the keeper of the Destiny Blade now. You will know when it is time to hand it on to another. As we drove the silver spears into the body of the Fiend, we drove a sliver of fear into all denizens of the dark, no matter how powerful. They now know what it is like to be afraid. And from the moment you sliced off the Fiend's head your destiny was changed. Where once you were hunted, now you have become the hunter of the dark!'

Then, without a backward glance, Grimalkin lifted the leather sack, threw it over her left shoulder and ran off into the night.

The Spook glanced at me sternly. 'Best take her words with a pinch of salt. The truth is that after your foolish pact, you were lucky to get another chance, lad,' he said, shaking his head. 'She's right on one count, though: there will be a final reckoning with the Fiend; until then we've bought ourselves a bit of respite. We need to put it to good use.'

CHAPTER
23
COVERED IN BLOOD

We stayed on at Shey's house while the buds on the hawthorn hedges burst into leaf and the sun coaxed the first reluctant spring flowers into bloom. Blustery winds still occasionally drove squalls of rain in from the west, but when the sun *did* shine, it had real warmth.

Good news had arrived from the County. As Grimalkin had predicted, both the Lowland and Highland Scots had joined a coalition of the free northern counties. A big battle had been fought north of Kendal. The enemy had been driven south, but the conflict was far from over yet. They had regrouped near Priestown, and another battle was imminent. Each day I waited expectantly, hoping for news. I wanted to go home.

The guards around the house had been doubled ever since one of them had mysteriously disappeared without a trace. I had noted Grimalkin's warning, but I had not seen any sign of the servants of the dark. The long war between the mages and the landowners had once more settled into the uneasy stalemate that had endured for centuries. Despite our best efforts, nothing had really changed.

Early one morning, with the sun shining in a cloudless sky, I was out exercising the dogs. I'd had an uncomfortable night and hadn't slept well. I'd been thinking about Alice. Her loss was a pain that still kept me awake.

The dogs sensed something first. All three of them stopped barking and came to a sudden halt. They were staring towards a wood about half a mile to the west. Suddenly, with Claw in the lead, they bounded away towards it, yelping excitedly. I called them back, but they ignored me, so I had no choice but to run after them.

I thought it was unlikely to be a rabbit or a hare. Claw, Blood and Bone were usually obedient dogs, and no matter how strong the scent they'd picked up, once given a command, they came to heel. What was wrong with them?

By the time I reached the trees, the dogs had already bounded far ahead, deep in the wood. I could hear their barks growing fainter and fainter. Annoyed, I slowed to a walk. Immediately I noticed that it was very quiet beneath the canopy of fresh green leaves. The breeze had died away and there was no birdsong. Nothing was moving. And then I heard it – the sound of distant pipes. I'd heard that music before. *It was Pan!*

I began to run. With every stride I took, the music grew louder. Moments later I burst into a clearing. The god had once again taken the form of a boy dressed in green, and was sitting on a log, a smile on his face. Around him stood a circle of bewitched animals: stoats, ferrets, rabbits, hares, along with my three dogs – all staring at him intently. Above, the branches were laden with birds. And there, at his feet, was a girl in a mud-splattered white dress.

She was lying on her back with her head resting against the log. Although young, her hair was white. It was not a pretty ash-blonde but the stark white of old age. She was wearing pointy shoes. With a shock, I suddenly recognized her: Alice.

Pan stopped playing and lowered his pipe. Immediately all the animals, with the exception of my dogs, fled into the trees. Above my head there was a beating of wings as the birds dispersed. Claw, Blood and Bone moved towards me and began to whine softly. Now that the music had stopped, they were afraid.

I stared at Alice, a mixture of thoughts and emotions churning within me. In part I was filled with joy. She was back, when I had never ever expected to see her again. But there was clearly something wrong, and I was alarmed.

Before I could say anything, Pan spoke. 'I did not

forget you, nor what you asked; so, in gratitude for freeing me from the body of the goat, I've brought your friend back,' he said in lilting tones. 'When you bound the Fiend, the walls of his domain were weakened and I was able to enter. What you did was brave but foolish. His servants are after *your* head now. Sooner or later they will take it.'

Contradictory emotions swirled within me: joy at having Alice returned to me; dismay at what had been done to her.

'What's wrong with her?' I murmured, kneeling beside her, my happiness tempered by the change I saw. I stroked her face, but she flinched away from me like a wild animal, her eyes filled with terror.

'She has dwelt in the Fiend's domain and seen things such as no living mortal should ever witness. No doubt she has been subjected to many torments too. I fear for her mind.'

'Will she ever recover?' I asked.

'Who can say?' answered Pan with a careless smile. 'I have done what I can. But dealing with the Fiend is one more thing I have to thank you for. Practitioners of dark magic the world over have been weakened by what you have accomplished. The mages will now lack the strength to bind me. I will be able to keep my magic for myself!'

He smiled again, and slowly began to fade from sight. For a few seconds he lingered as a ghostly transparent figure; then was gone. Within moments, the birds began to sing again and a breeze sighed through the trees.

I turned to the figure lying before me. 'Alice! Alice! It's me, Tom. What's happened to you?' I cried.

But she didn't respond and just stared at me, her eyes wide with fear and bewilderment. I tried to help her to her feet, but she snatched her hand away and scrambled up behind the log. Apart from her white hair, she looked like my friend, the Alice I remembered, but her mind seemed changed utterly. Had she any recollection of me? Did she even know her own name? It didn't seem so.

I leaned forward, grabbed her by the wrist and tried

to pull her to her feet. She lashed out at me with the nails of her left hand, scratching my right cheek and just missing my eye. I looked at her warily. What could I do?

'Come on, Alice!' I said, pointing through the trees. 'You can't stay here. Let's go back to the house. It's all right – you're back from the dark. You're safe now. And listen – we did it! We've managed to bind the Fiend!'

Alice stared at me sullenly but made no response. Short of dragging her along by force, there was only one thing I could do. I turned to the dogs.

'Bring Alice back! Bring Alice!' I cried, pointing at her and then in the direction of Shey's house.

The three wolfhounds stealthily moved behind her and growled. Alice looked back at them, her face twitching with alarm. It pained me to have to do this to her, but I had little choice. She was not open to reason and I had to get her to the house somehow.

For a moment she remained rooted to the spot. It wasn't until Claw gave a warning bark and bared her teeth that she started to move. So it was that they herded

Alice along like a stray sheep. It took a long time because she kept trying to break free and had to be brought back and forced in the right direction. It wasn't easy for the dogs, and they were in some danger themselves. Every so often she would snarl and lunge towards them with her razor-sharp nails.

It took over an hour to get her back to the house – a walk I could have accomplished in no more than fifteen minutes. Once there, I realized that my troubles had just begun.

'Her reason's fled,' said the Spook, 'and there's no guarantee that she'll ever be herself again. And is it any wonder? Some folks have been driven completely mad after just one glimpse of a creature of the dark; the poor girl's actually spent time in the domain of the Fiend. The outlook's not good, I'm afraid.'

Alice was cowering in a corner of the yard, surrounded by the three dogs. Every so often a glimmer of cunning flashed into her eyes and she struck out. Claw already had a bloody scratch just above her right eye.

'There's got to be some way to make her better,' I said.

The Spook shrugged. 'Shey has sent for the local doctor, but I suspect he'll be worse than useless, lad. What do doctors know about the dark and its power?'

'Maybe a witch could help?' I suggested, anticipating the Spook's reaction – which was a flicker of anger across his brow. 'I mean a benign witch, a healer,' I continued quickly. 'There are a few back in the County. There's her aunt, Agnes Sowerbutts.'

'We'd have to *get* back to the County first,' said the Spook.

I nodded. It wasn't possible yet. I just hoped that the imminent battle would go our way and we would be able to return soon.

As the Spook had warned, the doctor wasn't any help. He merely left some medicine to make Alice sleep. At dusk we tried to dose her, but it wasn't easy. We needed the assistance of three of Shey's maids to hold her down. Despite that, she spat out the first three mouthfuls. Then they held her nose, forcing her to swallow. Once she was asleep they put her to bed and we locked the door of her room.

I awoke suddenly, aware that something was wrong. Immediately I heard the noise of pointy shoes crossing a wooden floor and I sat bolt upright. Alice's room was next to mine.

Quickly I climbed out of bed and pulled on my shirt, breeches and boots. I tapped on Alice's door before turning the key, which had been left in the lock. The bed was empty and the sash window had been opened wide so that a cold draught was lifting the curtains and gusting directly into the room.

I dashed over to the open window and peered out. There was no sign of Alice. The bedroom was only one floor up, so I climbed through the window, dropped onto the cinder path below and sprinted out across the garden. I called Alice's name softly to avoid waking the household. Her wildness had disrupted things enough already and I didn't want to put a further strain on Farrell Shey's hospitality.

Then, in the distance, I saw the silhouette of a girl – but she was not where I expected her to be. Alice hadn't made for the gate. She had climbed the garden wall and was almost over it!

I ran towards her, but long before I got there she was over the top and out of sight. Where was she going? I wondered. Anywhere just to get away? I reached the wall and started to climb. My first attempt was unsuccessful. There were few handholds and the rain had made the stone slippery, so I ended up falling back and landing awkwardly. Alice had made it look so easy. The second time, I managed to scramble quickly up onto the top of the wall. I'd just come close to twisting my ankle so I wasn't taking any chances: I turned round carefully, holding on tight and lowering my body before dropping down into a cobbled yard. I rolled over once but came to my feet quickly and peered out into the darkness, trying to locate Alice.

There was no moon and I had to rely on starlight. But even though I could see in the dark better than most other people, I could catch no sign of Alice.

So I concentrated, closed my eyes and listened.

Directly ahead I heard a shriek, and then a sort of scuffling and flapping. I ran towards the sound. There were more squawks, and I realized that the sounds were coming from the large wooden coop where Shey kept his chickens.

The nearer I got, the louder the noises erupting from the pen. The birds were fluttering about in panic.

With a strong sense of unease, I recalled a dark memory from my childhood. One night, a fox had raided my dad's henhouse. When we arrived, bleary-eyed, forced from our beds by a terrible cacophony of sounds, five were already dead. Blood and feathers were everywhere.

But this time it wasn't a fox terrorizing the chickens – it was Alice. I couldn't see her, but even above the squawking of the birds I could hear something so grotesque that at first my mind refused to accept what it was. I crouched down close to the wooden pen, frozen to the spot. Then I heard shouts and the thud of heavy boots running towards us. Next thing I knew, someone was holding up a flaming torch to reveal the horror within.

Alice was on her knees in the middle of the coop; she was surrounded by dead and dying birds. Some had had their heads or wings torn off. One headless chicken was still running around. She held a dead bird in each hand. She'd been eating them raw, and her mouth was covered in blood.

CHAPTER 24
POOR TOM

Alice was a predator, no better than a wild animal filled with blood lust. It shook me to the core to see her behaving like this. The Spook was right: her mind was completely unhinged. Did any part of the Alice I'd known still remain, or was she now a total stranger?

The guard holding the torch swore. Another lifted a club and made to enter the pen. Alice lurched to her feet, and for a moment I thought she was going to attack him. But then she jumped. It was an impossible leap that sent her soaring right over his head, and over the gate behind him, to land in the mud outside. Then, without a backward glance, she ran off into the darkness.

I took one look at the startled faces of the guards, then turned and followed her. She was heading for the unguarded gates, and although I was sprinting, desperate to catch her, she seemed to be possessed of an unnatural strength. Alice was pulling away from me with every stride, and the sound of her pointy shoes hitting the grass was becoming fainter and fainter.

Soon my breath was rasping in my throat and I began to tire. I slowed down and continued in the same direction. Surely she couldn't keep that pace up for much longer, I thought. Every so often I halted, paused and listened. But there was nothing to be heard – only the sighing of the wind in the trees and the occasional eerie cry of some nocturnal creature. But then, at last, the crescent moon came up and I was finally able to employ some of the tracking skills the Spook had taught me. Soon I found Alice's footprints on the edge of a copse, confirming that I was still on her trail.

It wasn't long before I began to feel uneasy. Normally I'd never have ventured out without my staff, but I'd been so worried about Alice that I'd followed her instinctively, without thinking. As for the Destiny Blade, I'd left it in the sheath that Grimalkin had made. My silver chain was back in my bag and I hadn't even filled my pockets with salt and iron. I was completely unarmed – and cold too in just my shirt and breeches. I was completely unprepared, and each step I took away from the house could well be increasing my danger. Hadn't I been warned that the denizens of the dark would be after me in revenge for the part I'd played in binding the Fiend! While I tracked Alice, something could well be hunting *me*.

Alarmed by that possibility, I halted and slowly turned through a full circle, searching my immediate surroundings. I could neither see nor sense anything. There was no feeling of cold warning me that something from the dark was near. So, still nervous and very vigilant, I continued on my way. I couldn't leave Alice alone out here, whatever the risk.

Another hour passed, and I found more indications that I was still on the right track. As well as another set of footprints, I spotted a piece torn from Alice's dress as she'd walked straight through a patch of brambles. At least the shape and depth of the prints told me that she was no longer running, so I hurried on, hopeful of catching her at last. I continued until I reached the edge of a wooded hill.

The next set of prints I found made my heart plunge right down into my boots. There were some that didn't belong to Alice. There was also evidence of a struggle, the ground churned to mud – and spotted with blood. From the marks, I estimated that Alice had been seized by a group of people.

I felt so foolish – an apprentice spook with no weapons! – but how could I abandon Alice now? So I moved cautiously into the trees, came to a halt and listened. There was a deep and utter silence. It was as if everything was holding its breath. Slowly, trying not to make the slightest noise, I took another few steps then listened again. Silence. I felt increasingly uneasy.

I had to think quickly. I needed to improvise. On the ground to my left lay a fallen branch. I picked it up and was pleased to find that it was sound, and slightly thicker and longer than my staff; it was better than nothing. I hurried on, the incline becoming steeper with every step I took.

As I neared the summit of the hill, I sensed some unseen person watching me. However, the first eyes I saw weren't human. I looked up. The trees above were full of crows. I noted their sharp beaks and glossy black feathers, the razor-sharp claws cutting into the branches. My heart began to beat faster. Was the Morrigan here? I wondered. The birds were still, but when I lowered my gaze, I saw something that made my mouth go dry with fear.

Directly ahead of me, a man was sitting on the ground with his back against a tree trunk. He seemed to be staring at me, but his eyes were dark hollows. I took a step towards him, then another. With a shock I realized that he was dead. His damp, mildewed clothes were green, which marked him out as one of Shey's guards. It had to be the man who'd gone missing about a week earlier. He had been tied to the tree and his eyes had gone. The crows had feasted already.

At least this man was now dead and beyond further pain. And there was no sensation of cold to tell me that his spirit still lingered nearby. No, the cold only gripped me when I continued beyond him towards the next tree. Alice was sitting there in the same position, back against the trunk, wrists tied to it with twine, forced upwards at an angle of forty-five degrees. The bindings were very tight – I could see them cutting into her flesh. Additionally, her snow-white hair had been twisted into a knot and nailed to the tree, pulling her neck round at an awkward angle. She was moaning softly.

I rushed towards her and saw the blood congealed on the twine. She looked up at me then. Her eyes were still there, but they saw no more than the empty sockets of the dead man. She gazed right through me as if I didn't exist. When I knelt down before her, she whimpered. Her whole body was trembling. I touched her brow gently. How could I untie her arms without hurting her?

'Alice,' I said softly. 'I'm so sorry. I'll try to help but this might hurt a little . . .'

Suddenly the sensation of cold down my spine intensified. Something from the dark was approaching.

'Try feeling sorry for *yourself*, boy!' someone shouted behind me. 'Soon *you'll* be hurting too!'

I whirled round, recognizing the voice, and came face to face with the witch, Scarabek; Konal was now strapped to her back, his strangely ancient features leering at me over her shoulder. Behind her stood half a dozen bearded mages armed with swords. I heard sounds to my left and right: more armed men were walking towards me out of the trees. I was completely surrounded.

'Seize him!' the witch commanded.

Mages rushed forward, and I struck out at the nearest with the branch, brandishing it frantically to make him keep his distance. But it was useless against men with swords. Two cuts and I found myself holding just a short wooden stump in my hand.

'Drop it, or the next cut will sever your arm!' the nearest mage warned.

I obeyed and tossed it away, and was immediately seized roughly, my arms twisted painfully behind my back. I was then dragged towards the tree opposite Alice and pushed down into a sitting position so that I was facing her. Scarabek loomed over me.

'The goddess Morrigan is angry!' she cried. 'You have dared too much! You weakened her in the Hollow Hills, and she will not forget it. Since then you have bound the Fiend – a deed that has hurt all those who serve the dark. For that, she commands that you shall die a slow, painful death. Not for you the quick death of my loyal husband, Shaun. We shall tie you to this tree and let the Morrigan's crows peck out your eyes. After that we will cut you away piece by piece, starting with your fingers. We will sever them knuckle by knuckle, a morsel for each hungry beak that waits above! We will strip the flesh from your bones until only your skeleton remains! Bind him to the tree!' she ordered.

I fought with all my strength, but there were simply too many of them. They ripped the sleeves from my shirt, then held me against the trunk and pinned my arms back around it. Twine was bound very tightly about each wrist, and my arms were almost wrenched from their sockets as the two ends were pulled together and knotted behind the tree. It took all my willpower to stop myself from crying out. I didn't want to give Scarabek the satisfaction of knowing that I was in pain.

I looked up and saw the witch standing before me. 'My Shaun is dead because of you,' she snarled. She was holding out her left wrist like a falconer. But it wasn't a falcon that was perched there. It was a huge black greedy-eyed crow, its beak agape.

'We'll start with the left eye first,' she said.

Then, from behind her, someone else spoke. It was Alice.

'Poor Tom!' she cried. 'Poor Tom's hurt!'

'Aye, girl,' said Scarabek, turning to sneer at her. 'He's hurt, all right, but this is only the beginning.'

The crow unfurled its wings and flew onto my left shoulder. I felt the sharp pressure of its claws as the cruel eyes stared into mine. I tried to turn my head away, but it hopped nearer and its beak jabbed at my left eye.

CHAPTER 25
THEY ALL FALL DOWN

I squeezed my eyes shut and leaned as far away as possible, twisting my head to make it difficult for the crow to reach its target. But I knew it was useless. Within moments I'd be blind.

Suddenly Scarabek shrieked, and I felt the crow relax its sharp grip on my shoulder. The pressure was gone. Had the ugly bird flown away? I wondered. I opened my eyes cautiously and, to my surprise, saw it lying on the ground at my side. It wasn't moving. Its eyes were wide-open but looked like glass. What was wrong with it? Was it dead?

'Tom's hurt!' cried Alice again. 'Don't hurt him any more!'

The witch was staring down at the dead crow, a look of incredulity on her face. Then she turned to Alice. 'You!' she cried. '*You* did that!'

'Ain't right that you hurt Tom,' Alice retorted. 'He don't deserve that. Why don't you try picking on me instead?'

Scarabek pulled a knife from her belt and took a step towards Alice. 'I'll do just that, girl!' she said with a snarl. 'I'll attend to you myself!'

'You can't hurt me,' Alice told her. 'You ain't strong enough.'

A couple of the mages laughed, but not that heartily. Bound to the tree and helpless, taunting a witch armed with a knife, Alice's words seemed insane. Her pretty features were twisted into a sneer – the expression I'd seen on the face of her mother, Bony Lizzie, before she cast some dark, malevolent spell.

Then I felt it. It was as if someone had stabbed a shard of ice into my spine. That chill always warned me that something from the dark was close – I'd felt it as the witch and the mages had approached. But this had a strength and intensity beyond anything I'd experienced before.

And then, to my astonishment, Alice ripped her hands free of the twine that bound her to the tree, reached up to pull her hair clear of the nail and stood to face the witch. There was blood dripping from her lacerated wrists, but she didn't seem to feel any pain. She was smiling, but it wasn't a pretty smile. It was filled with malice. Scarabek hesitated and lowered her blade.

Then Alice turned back, bending her head down towards the tree trunk. What was she doing? When she turned to face the witch again, however, she was scowling.

Scarabek gave a sudden shriek of anger and ran straight at her, knife raised. I didn't see what happened next because she was obscuring my view of Alice. But she suddenly threw up her hand and gave a cry of pain, then stumbled to her knees. Alice laughed hysterically as Scarabek twisted towards me and staggered to her feet again.

The witch seemed to have forgotten all about Alice. She was now approaching me very slowly, unsteadily. But she was still holding the blade and her intent was clear. I noticed the mages staring at her with looks of utter horror on their faces. She was going to cut me – no doubt keeping a thumb-bone for herself. I was terrified.

But then I glanced up at her face and immediately saw why she had screamed. A nail had impaled her green left eye, and blood was running down her cheek. Alice must have pulled the nail out of the trunk with her teeth and had spat it into the witch's eye with great force and accuracy.

Scarabek staggered again, still lurching towards me. As she did so, Konal gave a blood-curdling squeal. Whether mortally wounded or not, the witch still had enough life in her to wield the blade. It seemed as though nothing could save me.

Then I heard a rumble from somewhere deep within the ground, and all at once the whole world began to move. Above my head the branches bounced and writhed as if the tree trunk was being twisted and shaken by a giant's hand. The witch's gaze left me and she glanced upwards fearfully. But the danger came from the other direction.

A huge crack suddenly opened in the earth. With a grinding, splintering roar, it gaped wider, moving towards Scarabek faster than a person could run. At the very last moment she tried to leap clear, but it was too late. The earth swallowed her up and closed with a deep reverberating thud, leaving only the fingers of her left hand visible.

With harsh cries, the flock of crows quickly took flight; then the ground beneath my feet began to buck and shake, and the surface became as liquid as an ocean, with waves rolling across the forest floor. They seemed to be radiating from where Alice was standing, and even above the noise I could hear her chanting a spell in the Old Tongue. Mages and their servants were now running in all directions.

The trees were leaning at crazy angles, their roots dislodged by the violent movement. Then, suddenly, everything became still and quiet again, as if the whole world was holding its breath, appalled at what had happened. Now there was only one thing moving; one new sound to fill the silence.

Alice was spinning, dancing across the grass with her arms extended, blood still dripping from her wrists. Her eyes were closed, and she was smiling and humming something under her breath. She spun faster and began to sing just loud enough for me to hear the words:

'A ring a ring of roses, a fist full of thorns,
A ring a ring of roses, a head full of horns.
I'll give a laugh and then a frown
So they all fall down!'

She giggled and repeated the last line as if it pleased her: *'So they all fall down!'*

At that, Alice seemed to lose her balance, and fell down hard, giggling. Then she put back her head and laughed loudly, and it was a long time before she

343

stopped. Finally she was quiet, and a solemn expression settled upon her face. She began to crawl towards me, coming so close that our faces were almost touching.

'I can make 'em all fall down, Tom. Ain't that true? Even Grimalkin, the strongest of 'em all – I could do it to her too. Don't you believe me?'

She was staring intently into my eyes. I nodded in agreement, simply to humour her. My wrists were still burning and throbbing, and I felt as if I was going to be sick any moment, the bile rising in my throat.

Alice now moved her head up and brought her mouth close to my left hand. She gripped the twine binding my wrist with her teeth and bit through it. I gasped with pain. Then she did the same to my right wrist.

I lowered my arms, relieved to be free. No matter what dark powers Alice had used, at that moment I truly didn't care. I had my life back when I thought I'd lost it.

Next Alice circled my left wrist with her fingers and

thumbs. There was a sudden sharp pain, followed by a tingling sensation that radiated from her thumbs to my fingers and then up through my wrist and arm. And the throbbing pain began to lessen. She did the same to my right wrist, then leaned down and put her arm round my back, easing me to my feet.

'Think you can walk, Tom?' she asked.

I nodded.

'Then it's best we get away from here. The ones who got away won't stay scared for ever. They're mages and used to dealing with the dark.'

I stared at Alice. Apart from the colour of her hair, she seemed almost back to normal. 'Are you better, Alice?' I asked.

She bit her top lip and shook her head. Her eyes brimmed with tears. 'Better? I'll never be better now, Tom. But I want to be with you. I want that more than anything else in the world. It's what's just saved us both.'

I sighed and shook my head. 'We need to talk about all this. Where did you get the power to do that?'

'Not now, Tom. I need some time. We'll have no peace when we get back – not after all that's happened – but come to my room tomorrow night and I'll tell you what I can. Is it right what you said yesterday? Did you really manage to bind the Fiend?' she asked me.

I nodded. 'Yes, it's true. We're free again, Alice.'

She smiled and took my hand. 'So we have a little time, Tom – a little breathing space to think of a way to sort him out once and for all.'

I frowned. 'But the first thing is to get back to Shey's house,' I said. 'After that business in the chicken coop I doubt we'll be welcome there any more. You do remember what happened there . . . ?'

Alice nodded sadly. 'I remember everything,' she said. 'I'll try and explain tomorrow.'

As we set off, I looked back. Four or five crows were pecking at something on the grass. One took flight, swooping low over us before soaring up to land on a branch. In its beak it was holding one of the dead witch's fingers.

I gripped Alice's hand even more tightly. It was good to be together again.

Back at the house, it took all my powers of persuasion to deflect Shey's anger from Alice; but, with the Spook's help, he and his men were finally persuaded that she had been under the influence of a spell, but was now restored to her old self.

With that first crisis over, we decided not to tell the Spook anything for now. I knew he was wondering what had really happened, but realized that this was not the time to question us closely.

We didn't even have the problem of explaining away the lacerations to our wrists. By the time we reached the house they were almost completely healed – with no scars to show what had been done to us. Healing was a benign act, but the exercise of such extreme power could only have come from the dark. Exhausted though I was, I slept little for the remainder of that night.

In the morning there was news of the war brought by a despatch rider from Dublin.

The Spook came to tell me himself:

'Good news, lad, really good news. The enemy have been defeated in a big battle north of Priestown and have fled in disarray to the very southern border of the County. They are now in full retreat. We can go home, lad, back to the County. I can rebuild my house and start to collect and write books for a new library!' There were tears glistening in his eyes; tears of hope and joy.

But despite that good news, I dreaded my forthcoming talk with Alice. What had happened to her in the dark? What had she become? Why could she never be better again? Was she a malevolent witch at last? The way she had slain our enemies the previous night made it look that way.

After everyone had gone to bed and the house was quiet, I went to talk to Alice. This time I didn't bother to rap on her bedroom door. She was expecting me, and I certainly didn't want to risk waking the Spook, whose room was just a little way down the corridor.

She was sitting on the edge of the bed, staring

through the window into the darkness. As I entered the room, softly closing the door behind me, she turned towards me and smiled. I picked up the candle from the dressing table and set it on the window ledge. Next I drew up a chair and sat down facing her.

'How are you feeling?' I asked.

'All right, Tom. Leastways, I ain't too bad as long as I don't think about what's happened.'

'Do you want to talk about it? Would that help or just make it worse?'

'Whether I want to talk about it or not ain't the point, Tom. You deserve to know it all. Then you've got to decide if you still want to be my friend.'

'Whatever you tell me, I'll still be your friend,' I told her. 'We've been through too much together to go our separate ways now. And we need each other to survive. But for you I'd be dead now – cut to pieces by that witch and fed to the crows.'

'What I did I can't undo. And I wouldn't if I could – otherwise I'd have lost you for ever, and lost my own life too. *But I liked it, Tom.* That's the horror. I enjoyed

349

destroying that witch. Whenever I hurt or killed something from the dark before, I felt sick afterwards, but not this time. I liked testing my strength against hers. I liked winning. I've changed. I'm like Grimalkin now. That's how she feels. She loves a fight! I killed – and I didn't care!'

'Is it because you've spent so long in the dark, do you think?' I asked, keeping my voice low. 'Is that what's changed you?'

'Must be, Tom, and I can't help it. When I came back from the dark, I didn't think it was real at first. I thought I was still there. That's why I was scared and shrank away from you. Those who served the Fiend often played tricks like that on me. Once before, I thought they'd sent me back to our world. I saw you at the edge of a wood. Really thought it was you too. You smiled at me and squeezed my hand. But it was just a trick. You slowly turned into a devil. I watched your face warp, and twisty horns start to sprout from your forehead. And I realized that I hadn't left the dark at all. So I thought what Pan said was just another trick and the same was going to happen again. I thought you were just a devil with a human face.'

I nodded. I had thought Alice was insane, but what she said made perfect sense. It would be the natural reaction of somebody who thought that the world wasn't real; that it was an illusion created by the dark to torment her.

'But how did you know it was me this time?' I asked. 'Even though they tied me to the tree and were about to kill me, it could still have been a trick.'

'When I was trapped in the dark, the devil that pretended to be you had his arms covered. But here, as soon as they ripped your sleeves off, I saw my brand on your arm, Tom. That mark is very special to me and you – it couldn't be faked even by the Fiend himself!'

The scars she'd left on my arm had never faded. It was her special brand that marked me as belonging to her and no other witch.

I nodded, but then thought of something else. 'But what about the chicken coop, Alice? What about that? Why did you do that?'

Alice shivered, so I leaned forward and put my arm around her shoulder. It was a long time before she answered.

'I'd only thought to escape and was heading for the wall. But then I smelled the warm blood pumping through their veins and I couldn't help myself. It was a terrible urge to drink blood. Being in the dark has changed me, Tom. Ain't the same, am I? I think I belong to the dark now. What if I can't cross running water any more? Old Gregory will know what I am instantly!'

This was really worrying. If my master had firm proof that Alice was a dark witch, he'd bind her in a pit for the rest of her life; no matter how good a friend she'd proved, he would do what he thought was his duty as a spook.

I thought back to the words Mam had once spoken about Alice:

She was born with the heart of a witch and she's little choice but to follow that path.

But then Mam had gone on to say that there was

more than one type of witch: Alice might turn out to be benign rather than malevolent. The third possibility was that she would end up somewhere between good and evil.

That girl could become the bane of your life, a blight, a poison on everything you do, she had told me. *Or she might just turn out to be the best and strongest friend you'll ever have.*

In my mind there was no doubt that the latter was true. But was it possible that Alice could become a malevolent witch and *still* be my ally? Wasn't that true of Grimalkin?

But I had one more question: 'Alice – where did you get all that power from? Is it because you were in the dark for so long?'

Alice nodded but she looked doubtful. For a moment I thought she was trying to hide something, but then she spoke slowly. 'I think I've brought power back from the dark' – she paused and looked at me – 'but I've always had more power than I've shown to you, Tom. I was warned by someone not to use it – to bury it deep inside me and try to forget it was there. Do you know why, Tom?'

I shook my head.

'Because each time you use such dark power, it changes you. Bit by bit you get closer to the dark, until eventually you are part of it. Then you've lost yourself and can never get back to what you once were.'

I understood. This was why the Spook feared so much for us both. I remembered something else Mam had once said to me when I told her how lonely my life as a spook was proving.

How can you be lonely? You've got yourself, haven't you? If you ever lose yourself, then you'll really be lonely.

I hadn't fully understood her words then, but now I did. She meant the integrity, the spark of goodness within you that makes you who you really are. Once that was extinguished, you were lost and truly alone, with only the dark for company.

Once again, I've written most of this from memory, just using my notebook when necessary.

Tomorrow we begin our journey back to the County. The first stage is to cross Ireland. But many streams and rivers lie in our path. Will Alice be able to cross them? Only time will tell.

The Spook knows nothing of this, and he seems fitter, stronger and more cheerful than at any time during the past two years. We still have the majority of the money that we earned dealing with the jibbers in Dublin. My master says he is going to use it to start rebuilding his house, beginning with the roof, kitchen and library.

As for Grimalkin, so far we have heard nothing more from her. We can only hope that she managed to elude or slay her pursuers and that the Fiend's head is still safely in her possession.

In addition to my staff and silver chain, I now have a third weapon – the sword given to me by Cuchulain, the Destiny Blade. I will need its sharp edges to defend myself against the denizens of the dark, who will pursue me in revenge for binding the Fiend.

The time is fast approaching when I will no longer be an apprentice; I will be a spook, and I am determined to be every bit as good as my master. In addition to that, I am my mother's son, with the special gifts that she has passed down to me. The dark may pursue me, but the time will come when what my mother foretold will come to pass. And as Mam and Grimalkin both prophesied, I *shall* become the hunter, and they will run from *me*. My time is coming, and that day is not very far away.

War will have changed the County for ever, but there'll still be the dark to fight. I just hope that my family has survived.

Despite all that's happened, I'm still the Spook's apprentice and we're on our way back to Chipenden. We are going home at last.

Thomas J. Ward

READ ON FOR A PEEK AT THE BRAND-NEW
TITLE IN THE WARDSTONE CHRONICLES
AVAILABLE JUNE 2012 . . .

SPOOK'S
BLOOD

'I am Siscoi, the Lord of Blood, the Drinker of Souls!
Obey me now or you will suffer as few have suffered.'

Time is running out for Thomas Ward. His final battle
against the Fiend is drawing near, and the Spook's
apprentice has never felt more alone in his task.

Isolated and afraid, the Fiend is set to send the
greatest of his servants against him – Siscoi, a Vampire
God more ferocious than anything he has yet faced.
Tom must risk his life to prevent the evil beast from
entering this world, even as he learns that the final
destruction of the Fiend may involve a sacrifice more
terrible than he can imagine . . .

CHAPTER 1
TIME TO REBUILD

The Spook was perched on a log in his garden at Chipenden, the sun singing through the trees and the air bright with birdsong. It was a warm spring morning in late May – as good as it got in the County. Things seemed to be changing for the better. I was sitting on the grass wolfing down my breakfast and he was smiling to himself and looking quite contented for a change as he gazed back towards the house.

From it came the sound of sawing; I could smell the sawdust. My master's house was being repaired, starting with the roof. It had been burned out by enemy soldiers, but now the war in the County was over, and it was time to rebuild and get on with our lives as a

Spook and his apprentice dealing with all manner of things from the dark – boggarts, ghosts, ghasts and witches.

'I can't understand why Alice would leave like that without saying anything,' I complained to the Spook. 'It's not like her at all. Especially as she knows we'll soon be setting off east and will be away for at least a couple of days.'

My friend Alice had disappeared three nights earlier. I had been talking to her in the garden and had left briefly to tell the Spook something, saying I'd be back in a few moments. On my return she had gone. At first I hadn't been too worried, but then she'd missed supper and hadn't reappeared since.

The Spook sighed. 'Don't take this too hard, lad, but maybe she's gone for good. After all, you've been bound together for quite some time by the need to use that blood jar. Now she's free to do as she pleases. And she's a different person after being dragged off to the dark and held there for so long.'

My master's words were harsh. Despite the fact that

she had been helping us for years, he still didn't trust Alice. She'd been born in Pendle and had spent two years being trained as a witch; John Gregory would be glad to see the back of her. When we were in Greece, Alice had created a blood jar to keep the Fiend at bay; otherwise we would both have been snatched away into the dark. Now it was no longer needed. We had bound the Fiend and cut off his head – which was now in the possession of Grimalkin, the witch assassin. She was on the run from his servants. Were the two halves of his body ever reunited, he would be free again and his vengeance would certainly be terrible. The consequences would be dire, not only for the County, but for the whole world beyond it; a new age of darkness would begin. But we had bought a little time in order to seek a way to destroy him permanently.

My master's final words hurt me most of all. The Fiend had taken Alice off into the dark; on her return she'd changed dramatically. Her hair had turned white: that was merely physical, but I feared that her soul had been damaged – that she'd moved closer to the dark.

Alice had expressed that same concern. Maybe she would never return? Maybe she could no longer be close to a spook's apprentice? After four years of facing dangers together, we had become close friends and it saddened me that we were now drifting apart. I remembered something my dad had told me when I was younger. Although just an ordinary farmer, he'd been wise, and as I was growing up he'd taught me lots of truths about life.

'Listen, Tom,' he'd once said. 'You have to accept that in this world things are constantly changing. Nothing stays the same for ever. We have to learn to live with that.'

He was right: I'd been happy living at home with my family. Now Mam and Dad were both dead and I could never go back to that life. I just hoped that my friendship with Alice wasn't coming to an end too.

'What sort of place is Todmorden?' I asked, changing the subject. There was no point in arguing with my master about Alice.

'Well, lad, my duties have never taken me to that

town but I do know a bit about it. Todmorden straddles the eastern County border, which is marked by the river Calder. So half the town is in the County and half is beyond it. No doubt the folk across the river will have different customs and attitudes. We've travelled a bit in the past two years – firstly to Greece, next to the Isle of Mona, and finally to Ireland. Each of those lands presented us with new problems and difficulties to overcome. The fact that our destination isn't far from home doesn't change the fact that we need to be on our toes.'

The Spook's library had been destroyed in the fire – the legacy of generations of spooks, filled with knowledge of how to fight the dark. Now we had heard of a collection of books about the dark in Todmorden. After ringing the bell at the withy trees crossroads late one night a week earlier, a mysterious visitor had left a note for us. It had been short but to the point:

Dear Mr Gregory,
I learned with deep sadness of the loss of your Chipenden

library. I offer my condolences. However, I hope to be of assistance because I own a large collection of books about the dark. Perhaps some might be of use to you? I am prepared to sell at a reasonable price. If you are interested, please visit me soon at Todmorden. I live in the house at the top of Bent Lane.

Mistress Fresque

Only one book from my master's original library remained – the Bestiary that he had written and illustrated himself. It was more than just a book. It was a living, working document annotated by his other apprentices – including me. It was a record of his life's work and what he had discovered with the help of others. Now he hoped to start restocking his library. However, he refused to take any books from the small collection in the watermill north of Caster that had been occupied by Bill Arkwright, one of his ex-apprentices. He had hopes that one day the mill would become a spook's house once more; if that happened, the new incumbent would need those books. John

Gregory anticipated that the visit to Todmorden would be the first step to replacing his own library.

My master had originally intended to set off right away but, as interested as he was in acquiring books, the rebuilding of his house came first, and he had spent hours going over plans and schedules with the builder. He had a list of priorities, and the completion of a new library to house books was one of them. I'd encouraged him in that because I wanted to delay our departure to give Alice time to return.

'What's the point of getting new books if we haven't a library ready to put them in?' I'd argued.

He'd agreed, and it had bought me more time, but at last we were off to meet Mistress Fresque.

In the afternoon, about an hour or so before we were to set off on our journey, I wrote a note of my own. This one was for the absent Alice:

Dear Alice,
Why did you go off like that without a word? I

am worried about you. This morning my master
and I will set off for Todmorden to look at the
library we heard about. We should be back in a
couple of days.

Take care. I miss you.

Tom

But no sooner had I pinned it to the new back door
than I suddenly sensed a coldness – the warning I
sometimes get that something from the dark is nearby.
Then I heard someone coming up behind me. My staff
was leaning against the wall, so I snatched it up and
spun round to face the danger, holding it in the
defensive diagonal position.

To my surprise, Alice was standing before me. She
was smiling but looked tired and dishevelled, as if
she'd been on a long wearisome journey. The coldness
quickly faded. She wasn't an enemy, but that brief
warning worried me. To what extent had she been con-
taminated by the dark? I wondered.

'Alice! I've been really worried about you. Why

did you leave like that without saying anything?'

She stepped forward and, without answering, gave me a hug. After a few moments I held her at arm's length.

'You look like you've had a hard time of it, but it's really good to see you,' I told her. 'Your hair's returning to its usual colour. It'll be back to normal soon.'

Alice nodded, but the smile slipped from her face and she looked very serious. 'I've something really important to tell you, Tom,' she said. 'It's best if Old Gregory hears it too!'

I'd have liked a little more time to talk to Alice alone, but she insisted that we see my master immediately. I went to fetch him, and as it was a sunny afternoon, he led the way to the bench in the western garden.

The Spook and I sat down but Alice remained standing. I had to stop myself from laughing because it reminded me of the occasions when Spook would stand there giving me a lesson while I took notes. Now my master and I were like two apprentices!

But what Alice had to say soon wiped the smile off my face.

'While she was on the run with the Fiend's head, Grimalkin took refuge in Malkin Tower,' she told us. 'It's a long story, and no doubt she'll eventually tell you the details of what happened herself—'

'Is the Fiend's head still safe in her possession?' interrupted the Spook.

'It's been hard, but Grimalkin's kept it safe so far. Ain't going to get any easier though. There's some bad news. Agnes Sowerbutts was killed by the Fiend's supporters.'

'Poor Agnes,' I said, shaking my head sadly. 'I'm really sorry.' She was Alice's aunt and had helped both of us in the past.

'One of the two lamia sisters was killed as well, and now only one – Slake – is left defending the tower. She's under siege and can't hold out indefinitely. From what Grimalkin said, it's important that you go there as soon as possible, Tom. The lamias studied your mam's books and found out that she was the one who hobbled the Fiend. Slake thinks that by looking more closely at the hobbling process you might be able to work out how to finish him off for good.'

The hobble had limited the Fiend's power in certain ways. If he was able to kill me himself, he'd reign on in our world for a hundred years before being forced to return to the dark. Of course, for an immortal being, that wasn't long enough. But if he got one of his children to do the deed, the son or daughter of a witch, then the Fiend could rule the world indefinitely. There was also a third way to achieve this end: he could simply convert me to the dark.

'I always thought it was likely that Mam did the hobbling,' I said. After all, I was her seventh son born to Dad, another seventh son, and thus her chosen weapon against the Fiend. The hobble concerned me, and which other of his enemies could have been powerful enough to do it?

The Spook nodded in agreement but didn't look at all happy. Any use of magic made him very uneasy. At present an alliance with the dark was necessary but he didn't like it.

'I thought the same,' said Alice. 'But there's one more thing, Tom. Whatever's needed, whatever it takes, you need to do it at Halloween. There's a seventeen-year cycle, and it's got to be next Halloween – the thirty-fourth anniversary of the hobble carried out by your mam. That leaves little over five months . . .'

'Well, lad,' said the Spook, 'you'd better get yourself to Malkin Tower as soon as possible. That's more important than books for my new library. Our visit to Todmorden can wait until you get back.'

'Aren't you coming?' I asked.

My master shook his head. 'Nay, lad, not this time. At my age the County damp starts to rot your joints and my old knees are playing up worse than I can remember. I'd only slow you down. With the girl to guide you, you'll be able reach the tower without being seen. Besides, you've got years of training behind you now; it's time you started to think and behave like the spook you'll soon become. I have confidence in you, lad. I wouldn't send you off like this if I didn't think you could take care of yourself.'

FIRE CITY
By Bali Rai

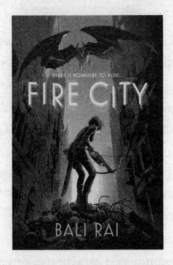

'Never talk in one spot for too long . . .
Fire City is full of people desperate enough
to sell their souls for a piece of bread'

Fire City is a lawless place – plagued by gangs
of zombies, and ruled in an uneasy alliance
between humans and demons.

Those who don't belong must fend for themselves.
They are hunted for sport each night or else are
taken prisoner by the demons and 'disappeared'.

Then, into this chaos comes fifteen-year-old Jonah, a
stranger with vengeance on his mind and secrets to hide . . .

ISBN: 978 0 552 55602 6

GRYMM
By Keith Austin

Something stirred in the gravelly yard beneath their window . . . A soft slippery nuzzle, the sort of sounds you'd expect a pig to make with its snout in a trough . . .

The small mining town of Grymm, perched on the very edge of the Great Desert, is the kind of town you *leave* – but when Dad gets a three-month contract in the town's mine, Mina and Jacob, unwilling stepbrother and sister, are reluctantly *arriving*.

From a grotesque letting agent who seems to want to eat their baby brother, a cafe owner whose milkshakes contain actual maggots and the horribly creepy butcher, baker and candlestick-maker, Mina and Jacob soon realize that nothing in Grymm is what is appears to be.

And then things get seriously weird when their baby brother disappears – and no one seems to even notice! In Grymm, your worst nightmares really do come true

ISBN: 978 1 849 41556 9

THE SPOOK'S WEBSITE

Visit the Spook's website to be the first
to find out all the latest news and previews
of Joseph Delaney's books.

- Read the author's blog
- Explore the County in an interactive map
- Upload scary pictures and play the Spook's Battle
- Regular competitions and features
- Register as a Spook's Apprentice for email newsletters

www.spooksbooks.com